NJAWARA BANTI YASSIN

I0657519

BY

DR. ALHASAN SISAWO CEESAY, MD

FIRST PRINTING

PUBLISH KUNSA.COM

ISBN 978-1-910117-41-5

INSCRIBED TO

My Parents, Wife and Children, Teachers, Friends, Colchester Friends of Manding Charitable Trust UK and Friends of Manding Alpena, Michigan, USA; and the downtrodden

The way to a man's heart is through his stomach but a bouquet of roses with a diamond engagement ring inserted in it is sure way to catch a girl's armour.

Dr. Alhasan S. Ceesay, MD

PREFACE AND ACKNOWLEDGMENTS

Every Gambian village has a romantic nook. Njawara boosts of a mythical romantic square called 'Banti Yassin' where love fumes and spells percolate. If youth is full of romance and blundering then manhood is a sea of struggles.

This work is based on true romantic events in families and stories depicted herein. These lovebirds came to their fondness in the most magical route imaginable. This romantic venture will sweep you off your feet as you browse the pages herein.

It is a story about people at their best towards others in partnership. The characters depicted represent no real people or anyone in particular; even if these may coincidentally be identical to someone a reader may know or identify with.

All efforts are in place to avoid revealing the actual people whose romantic stories are implied in this work. Rest assured that every line in this work and story about love is true about how these lovebirds went head over heel sailing in the wide Wild Ocean of tantalizing romance.

Njawara City, capital of Lower Badibou, the Gambia, has been chosen a stepping-stone for magnificent, sensual, ecstatic romantic stories. Hearts mentioned in this work are the envy of the Goddess of love. The stories dwarf the romantic scenes in the Arabian Knights and their stunning belly dancing maidens. Then here is fantasia to set you sailing into memorable love lane that could as well remind you days gone by. It is sure to bring envy and joyful tears out of you for the stories are pure love.

Without further ado, I will let you read along to quell your curiosity. Oh, by the way if your love one or companion, partner or call it whatever setups is away, I suggest you get a soft doll to squeeze and some popcorn to munch while browsing these pages.

Please allow me express profound gratitude to wife and children for being with me in thick and thin of this adventure to bring medical service to villagers; to the numerous friends who were persistent in encouraging me publish these epic romantic stories. In the mean time allow me express profound gratitude to my wife and children for bearing and persevering patiently through with me in thick and thin during my drive to bring medical aid and service to villagers. Also I am immensely thankful to illustrious lawyer Ousainu Darboe, Lorna Robinson, Eliza Jones, Dr. Laurel Spooner, Dr. Barbra Murray, Dr. Phil Spooner, Dr. Richard Murray, Dr. Malkaight Singh, Cloyd Ramsey, Howard Riggs, Rita Riggs, Dr. Charles Egli, Dr. Cooper Milner, Dr. Nelson Herron, Deidre O'Leary, Margaret Cruise, Bill Cruise, Alison

Cruise, Dr. Eunice Kahan, Dr. Betzabi Alison-Prager, Henry Valli, Fr. John Milner, Homer Shepard, Geraldine Shepard, Dr. Lamin J. Sisay, Dr. Sulayman S. Nyang, Bishops Masson & Coleman McGhee of the Episcopal Diocese of Michigan, Detroit, the Ceesay Committee Diocese of Michigan, Lois R. Leonard, Rev. Walter White, Rev Huge White, Patricia Koblynski, Ishfaue Ahmed, Imran Khurum Ahmed, Mohamed Nasir, Ahmed Nizami, Abdinnisir Hassan, Faisal Alim, Abdal Rhaseed Suguelle, Noora Sugulle, Mahmud Adam, Ganem Al Hadied, Abdullah Shahim, Asiya Qadri, Yusuf Ali, Daryl Gasson, Kostas Milliotis, and numerous others whose names are not mention but not forgotten.

I write to raise awareness of NGO Manding Medical Center at Njawara village and raise funds for the building of a village hospital at Njawara, the Gambia. It is my hope that you would be inspired to join our dream of providing medical aid and service to Gambian villagers and children in the North Bank region.

Purchasing this book or donating in cash or kind would help bring our dream to fruition of Manding Medical Centre for a much needed healthcare delivery and hope to villagers, especially children who frequently die prematurely from childhood diseases because of lack of medical service.

Together we can catch a dream for the villager and children. Log onto: www. Friends of Manding gambimed, to learn more about our self-help village health project Manding Medical Centre at Njawara. Portions of proceed from sale of this work go to support goals of Manding Medical Centre. In addition it will in due course offer scholarships to rural candidates wishing to read for a medical or an agricultural degree and return to serve in rural Gambia.

Dr. Alhasan S. Ceesay, MD

Chapter 1

Njawara, located in Lower Badibou District at the fringes of Gambia and Senegal, was one of the vibrant trading centers during the colonial epoch. In Njawara's heydays a square flanked by four nameless streets was rendezvous place were men watched ladies pass by. The place was named after Yassin Njie, one of the most stunning ladies residents at Njawara during the 1940s. It was in this area that beautiful Yassin sat to wait for the arrival of her knight in shining Armour to sweep her feet off the ground and gallop to the bridal world or love lane. Many a man clashed because of beautiful Yassin and her popularity in the region.

Hence the log she sat on became a living symbol of Njawara's many romantic love stories. Banti Yassin still connotes love, friendship, and mellows idolization. Many vied and clamored for attention of beauties like Fatou Bah, Hady Fallen, Emily Nying, Hady Chorr and Madan Cham, and Yama Njie just to name few queens of the day in 1940. Most men at Njawara had their first approaches from this unique square. Little did the ladies know how much intrigue and excitement were waiting for them while passing Banti Yassin. Handsome men sit on and pass judgment on the looks and features of these Njawara maidens.

We will together follow the story in the case of Ali Bahol and Binta Njie. Ali Bahol being a shy man was now ready to muster his strength and nerves after overcoming anxious moments, ventured to start a conversation with Binta Njie. He right away told her how much she meant to him with a trailing voice almost in silence for fear of being rejected. He asked that she stay for a moment and assured her how much that would mean to him and his peers. What ensued was beyond his wildest expectation. Binta Njie retorted by asking, "Why did you keep this marvelous feeling in you and never let me know sooner?" The old cock cleared its throat and crowed several mellow sounds as if to announce a miracle about to unfold at Banti Yassin. Binta in a philosophical tone told him that their meeting was tomorrow for them and that the past was dead and gone. This statement coming from a seemingly quite lady left Ali's head turning. He could not decipher it at the time. Binta clarified saying, "I want you to know that the future for us was just beginning. It could be a wonderful future if only you, Ali, would let it be, if only you would stop looking backward and just plan on the future with faith, hope and confidence."Ali listened as if dying of thirst for her words were life-giving cool, fresh and melodious to the ear. He asked Binta, "Do you love me?" To which she replied, "With all my heart, beloved and you must learn to accept it, too.

You have tortured yourself for keeping this feeling in your heart and not sharing it out of your chest with me." However, it was not too late as she was still a sphincter. Ali came closer to her and knelt beside her, his arms on his sides, avoiding being fresh, but his face was only a few inches from hers, and his eyes, desperate with pleading, with hope that wanted more than any to accept her assurance and love. Binta, quibbling told him quietly "I loved you and wants you snap out of darkness and fear you locked yourself for so long."

Now it was Binta's turn to lean forward, framed his face between her hands and set her mouth on his lips in a kiss that was tender and compassionate and deeply loving. For a long moment they clung or remained glued together, wordless, and her face wet with tears of joy not wholly her own. She could not believe she at long last got her man. The only one she had dreamt of on several occasions. She privately sang songs and wrote poems about him and even told her girl friends how she would turn worthless if this man fails to marry her. Ali's peers taken by surprise hesitated to break into that lovely moment with anything so worthless as mere admiration. He announced joyously to the fellows that Binta loves him and that he will delegate his elders to go and ask for her hand in marriage soon.

They ended the encounter in celebrative mood and each promised the other to follow village traditions and consultation of respective in-laws. Despite village life revolving simply or mostly of an agricultural or rural time Ali and his future wife would have to follow footsteps of yester years. Yes, back in African village setting tradition supersedes. This commences with education and guidance from parents, initiation, which connotes the day that child, was circumcised and inducted into manhood or womanhood. Proud parents sacrifice cattle, goat or sheep for food to mark festivity honoring as well as welcoming the adolescent to full adulthood. As tradition would have it, a son is then given his own house and now more than ever he gains respect from his peers and girls. Finally, he is expected to marry and procreate before the individual's return to our maker and reunion with our ancestors in the world beyond. The adolescence endures these rules before being recognized as rightful adults of society. From henceforth a son is given recognition primed with respect for tradition demands that his community treat him as an adult. The young adult now earns respect of his peers of all genders and can choose to marry as early as at the ripe-full age of twenty-one or later.

In times past and even in some quarters today, his bride would have been already chosen for him by his parents and their historic and long time family line friends and would be in-laws. Roughly 45% of village males have the cherished chance of selecting their first wife by themselves as in Ali Bahol's case.

Polygamy is an accepted part of rural life and most men marry two or four wives. Marrying more than one wife is neither a power status nor is it an imposition on females by males. It is all done through individual choice to paraphrase it. I guess the English would call this marriage sanctioned by handshake and true word of all concerned.

It is considered sacrilegious to wrong the family name and honor. So the future couples are usually advised by their parents not to defile themselves for any unsavory behavior by them would earn them a permanent stigma in their villages and among their comrades.

Parents, in the 1940s, did have the final say as to which bachelor their daughters may marry. It was believed that by so doing it helps in directing or preparing the children to who is an eligible bachelor acceptable to them and their parents.

Dr. Alhasan Sisawo Ceesay, MD

It may seem hash at a glance but upon deep reflection it was a great cure for curbing teenage pregnancies and teenage mothers abandoning innocent babies in street corners because of immaturity, lack of experience and responsibility of having brought some life that would need their support until when it too can be viable individual.

The above stand by villagers does not imply rigidity but simply a continuation of guidance and a practice that had worked well since the arrival or creation of Adam and Eve and has prevented lots of heartaches or women spending a lifetime without husbands. Deep down we all love and want to be loved and marriage was one successful sanctioned by society we lived in embraced.

Liberated or not, be fully aware that there is no miss or mr. right knight with shining amour ready to sweep us off our feet to the bridal world. In village life everything conforms to laws of nature or suicidal ends results such as drugs, crime, prostitution and alcohol would take over our intransigent decisions.

Village girls do not feel left out by having their husbands chosen in these situation, even where they may not end up being with their initial choice, for they have the blessings and backing of the social fabric.

Essential community or social ingredient input to our lives is on the verge of disappearing in this modern day life styles. Barring any reasonable alibis for annulments, Ali Bahol can now ask for Binta Njie's hand in marriage. It is now the duty of his father and uncles to meet the in-laws and discuss the required payments and dowry for Binta Njie. As a formality, the father or uncle of the gentleman sends his best friend with some cola nuts to talk to the parents of the bride and formally ask for the hand of the daughter (Binta Njies, in this case) in marriage to their son Ali Bahol. The matter is again thoroughly debated in the most cordial manner and any agreement reached becomes binding on both sides of the aisle. There will be no alteration of agreed dowry after a gentleman's handshake, which literally seals the deal for the couple and family. It is after this stage that the village town crier, then authorized to announce the good news, goes to homes asking elderly men and women to meet at the Mosque on a chosen Friday evening, in the event of a Muslim or Church to consummate the marriage between the intended couples. Now both Ali Bahol and Binta Njie's age group pitch in to help the preparation for the forth-coming wedding ceremony. The preparation may take six months to a year depending on the requested dowry by the bride's parents and how elaborate an affair the families wished.

When everything is met, all the adults in the village then converge and congregate in prayer to consummate the marriage at the mosque. Festivities are allowed only upon the completion of the mosque activities. Being found a virgin is a pride and self-fulfilling reward to village girls. It is guarantee of respect and trust from the onset of the marriage and an everlasting respect from her husband and community as well. Ladies found to be non-virgins are duped a disgrace to their families and friends. This concept is now fading away as the younger generation becomes educated and acculturated by the contacts with young foreign tourists and ideologies. In the day of the real marriage ceremony, the village and all the neighboring villages participate in the event. Binta Njie is dressed in the best bridal tradition costume and now addressed as "siet or manyo." There is always a whopping big marriage party with drumming and dancing all day until late in the evening before the bride finally enters her husband's house. The husband or his friends help her cross the so-called threshold. Then the friends leave them alone for the night. The nights and years to follow could never match ecstasy of this one. Now the couple stays permanently together, for better or for worse, as husband and wife.

The ceremony usually continues up to dawn before the younger celebrants' call it quit or retire to bed. The bride keeps on her bridal attire for at least two weeks before shedding them for good. Most women store these special dresses for life, giving them only to their daughters if these cannot get their own. Village ladies consent to be married but do not go around looking for husbands or playboys or getting involved in experiments, social exploits or freaky one night stands that only end of passing aids to its customers, as in other societies. Ali and Binta Njie-Bahol had five (three boys and two girls) lovely children. They lived happily until in their late eighties before returning peacefully to their maker.

Dr. Ceesay & Mr. Sisawo Ceesay Father, 1960

MEETING OF THE HEARTS

Kunsa Mori and his friends were at the Kinidima Restaurant in Banjul, capital of the smiling coast of Africa, eager to land the stimulus of the evening. They were in the midst of gentlemen's discussion when Kunsa saw a mesmerizing and what he later called the most tantalizing sumptuous looking figure cross the corner of his right eye. He looked over again and noticed a lovely young woman making her way towards him. The sight flabbergasted him, as he never saw a female of such bodily perfection matched by a face unrivaled by any of her age group. She was ravaging and sumptuous. Kunsa Mori became petrified and was hardly able to talk or return greetings this mirage of a lady gave. It was as if though he saw a maiden angel. He was struck by her beauty that made him turned his head several times to get a better look at her. She offered her hand in a friendly but none flirting manner to Kunsa who received it graciously in a semi stupor. Kunsa tried tidying himself, fixed his necktie and moved towards this mirage of beauty to share a word or two with her. She winked at him to enforce his confidence and asked that they select a table at a quieter corner of the restaurant. He did but as they sat facing each other in love without ever having uttered anything about their yearning to the other.

Kunsa opened the Pandora's box by saying, 'Ms, I will pay for the food and drinks you may choose and more'. This was confidence she was looking for in him. She smiled and leaned toward Kunsa, as if to grab him and swallow his lips instantly, and said, "I am Majula Seyabalo what is your real name"? Kunsa Mori struggled with himself as he tried to find a word or two to tell his simple name to the lady. He finally collected himself and said, "I am Kunsa Mori and I am in my final year at medical school. I am please to make the acquaintance of such ravaging beauty". Majula Seyabalo laughed in appreciation. Her pearly white teeth were dazzling and stupendously added her gorgeousness. Kunsa had fallen in love at the first glimpse of her and knew within him that he wanted this charming lady as a wife. Majula Seyabalo was twenty years old and five feet four inches and dons medium size breasts which alleys any normal male. Her body was of a stupendous perfect figure, not obese nor pencil shaped, and it petrified men like Kunsa who were not street savvy. Majula Seyabaloa was just a simple natural lady in control of her life and does not smoke, drink alcohol, dabble with leisure drugs or use the F-word as some loose bimbos pride themselves. She turned out to be one interested in family, motherhood, education, world affairs, work, charity and especially climate changes.

She said farmers like her were losing crops and arable land to farm because of hash changing weather. In short Majula Seyabalo makes one feel at ease in her presence and was gifted in picking one's brains, so to speak, as Kunsa would later confess to one of his colleagues at school. Majula was complete female envied by her contemporaries. While the waiter was busy filling up glasses, Majula asked Kunsa, "What job you like best"? Kunsa repeated, "I am currently a medical student but like my grandmother, I would like to spend the rest of his life practicing medicine in hinterland villages". Kunsa paused for a while, as if to gage Majula's reactions. Majula asked kunsa the thousand-dollar question in polite but serious manner. "Are you married, if not why not and what type of lady do you have in mind?" The whole evening at that moment swung toward an unfolding miracle of coincident for Kunsa. Kunsa found himself deeply in love with the figure before him who is almost asking him to propose therein and for good. He could not believe neither his ears, nor the body language and gaze from both of them. Mean while they have been stealing romantic glances at each other without letting the other notice. It was just ecstatic and very electrifying. They were strangers a few minute ago and now likely partners for life.

To make certain of her intent Kunsa threw the ball back at her by asking, "Please tell me what would make you betroth." First, she hesitatingly and in a shy way almost at low voice said, "Well I love simple, ambitious, hard working, caring and sharing and above a person of faith". Majula took great pain to avoid being the one that proposed as such is contrary to African tradition and makes the lady perceived a cheap stud, unintelligent scornful scum bat. Majula wants to maintain her respect and love of her husband and community. She continued by saying "I would like the man to love me as I am created and not to try to change me or any of my looks. The husband to be must accept the changes nature would bring forth as I age. I definitely like to have as many children as my husband wishes if not more but not less at any given time if health permits. I will do all I can to make him a good wife through our lives together. I will be a team member and would promote the family as long as she lives." The simplicity and candor of deliverance from this lady soon to be Kunsa' wife elated him to the point that he felt himself being at cloud nine and thankful that he met her in such unusual circumstances. It was love made in heaven and Kunsa held her hands in his for the first time since their rendezvous. Ruminating in Kunsa's head was a sense of being lucky comparing her with his female medical students he was so familiar with.

She was unique, very polite, almost too good to be true, and he believed she was made for him. She was the ideal partner he expected to marry after medical school. To strike a deal without saying it Kunsa asked Majula, "Do you like working with sick people in foreign or hinterland villages in Gambia?" She unhesitatingly told him, I was in fact thinking of going to Badibou and teach mathematics at a village school". This caused Kunsa to raise his glass and their hands crossed both toasted to African village experience as they downed their orange juices. Both continue the game of stealing affectionate glances amidst wide brim smiles in adoration of the other. Kunsa could not overcome his admiration of the perfect figure before him. Majula reiterated her previous question demanding an answer from Kunsa Mori. Kunsa reassured her by saying. " As far as I was concerned you are it and without you there would be no wife for me for life". He finally had the nerve to let her know how enamored he was and that he was definitely in love with her. He even stressed that he was not a little boy falling for faces but there was much in Majula that he would not allow himself to lose if she kindly and equally love him. At which juncture they held hands and gazed at each other in silence for three minutes or longer, only unbelievable romantic glances spoke, before Majula could utter a word.

Tears of joy welled from her eyes as she said "I love you with all my heart and soul and we are each other's comfort for better or for worse". Their pounding hearts relayed romantic depth of feeling and sincerity without a single word being spoken. Majula made certain she nailed him to her by asking, "Are you or do you have the same feeling for me as I have for you? Will you remain ever true to your words and to me and children we get in future?" Kunsa drew her closer and kissed her incessantly and she responded with eyes close to savor the yearning and not letting or wishing to relinquish his lips or tongue from her mouth. On lookers in the Restaurant applauded the lovebirds and wished them the best and continued affection for each other. That moment was worth millions of heavenly nights for both of them. While still embraced Kunsa asked her if that answered her question or clarified doubts she may have harbored. She looked at him and smiled again dazzling the place with her lovely ivory white teeth. A brief exchange of contacts i.e. telephone, mobile and even e-mails followed. The meal they ordered had to be kept warm for they had no time for food as their hearts were being filled to the brim with love made from heaven. They finally had few bites with each one trying to feed the other at whim. It was the best dinner either ever had since becoming adults.

They are now one of the happiest friends living on earth. The evening ended on good note for them. On that day both returned home, Kunsa driving Majula home and proceeded to his flat at Love Lane Square. No sooner than the time he opened his door the phone rang and the voice at the other end said "hello darling. I am already missing you. Do study but remember all work and no play make Jack a dull man. And I want you to pass so that we can go to practice medicine in Badibou." She added that she has decided to complete the Nursing training she started three semesters ago. She would let him know when she returns from the Nursing College the following morning. She reiterated her love, and threw in a goodnight kiss Kunsa relished. She asked that he call first thing in morning to make her day. It was all happening too fast for both, especially Kunsa whose only reason to step out of the Medical Library was to have a bite and relax with friends before returning to Gray's Anatomy and Harrison's Textbook of Medicine. He concluded that their' was love chemistry made by God and not alchemists. He would work hard to keep her and do his best at Medical School. The last phone conversation left him in cloud nine and he sang his heart out while taking shower. He came out and made a thick cup of coffee and amidst songs added milk to his heart's content.

They stationed at the desk to review until the wee hours before hitting the pillow. He set the alarm to wake him at 6:30 am for he has lecture at 8:00 am in the next building. The alarm rang as programmed and Kunsa jumped out of bed the happiest man in the planet and remembered to call Majula as was agreed upon last night. He pressed the fast dial key on his phone and very soon came Majula' melodious voice at the other end. "Good morning darling. Have you slept well? Thank you for calling. It has reinforced my trust in you being a responsible and caring man". This remark made Kunsa Mori very happy. Both promised to call the other after 5:00 pm for an update or what longing the other had. Majula went straight to the Admissions Office of Njawara Nursing College and requested application forms and the possibility of talking to an official. An appointment was booked for 1:00 pm for her to talk to student advisor Ms Jarala Nightingale. Majula Seyabalo filled all the forms, drew a cheque to cover the fees and presented all of it to Ms Nightingale who was very pleased to have her onboard and accepted all her transfer grades on her transcript. Nightingale told her that class start on the following Monday. Majula thanked the officer and joyfully rushed to tell Kunsa about her successes after 5:00 pm as agreed. She was determined never to interrupt him during school lecture hours.

Kunsa seem to simultaneously take the same attitude towards Majula. Hence he rang her 5 pm. "Hello love. How did your day go?" She told him of the good news of starting nursing classes the Monday coming.

 Kunsa bought a bouquet of red roses and had them delivered to her. You guessed right, like most women end up doing, Majula slept with the bouquet of roses clenched in her hand over her heart. She never had such peace of mind and she slept like a baby through the night.

Mean while Kunsa had one of his exams due in three days and Majula warned him not to call until after the exam and she would do likewise. This was true love for neither party wish to dislodge the other from their commitments.

Chapter 3

BUILDING A PROFESSION

Kunsa Mori redoubled his efforts at school while Majula Seyabalo let every word uttered by the nursing professors sink in her indelible spongy brain or mind. The lessons came back to her and she studied harder than she ever did at high school. Kunsa Mori and Majula vowed not to be intimate until their wedding day. In the mean time Majula rebuffed many suitors as soon they made any gestures. Medical school did not give Kunsa any time for girls and hence he had less problem of being snatched away. As far as he was concerned Majula would be much better partner and reward than most girls in his class. Alas, Kunsa sat for his exam on Friday leaving the weekend free for their rendezvous. He called promptly at 6.00 pm and asked Majula, "Darling, would like to join me for dinner at a restaurant of your choice?" Instead she decided to cook a delicious meal and took the food along for them to share at Kunsa's flat. Asked why she turned the table. She said, "We now have to learn to be thrifty with our monies as a lot depended on it". This touched Kunsa to the core for it proved he had not made wrong choice in allowing this girl of all girls into his heart and life. She was his quintessential love.

They however went to movies until 11.00 PM when Kunsa Mori took her back to her flat for she had assignments to complete during the weekend. She called as soon as Kunsa was about to retire to bed. Again they had what was one of their longest pillow chats as these were the epitome dream partners we all yearn to meet in our romantic days. Kunsa Mori asked Majula, "Is Njawara your hometown?" She replied, "It was not and that the rarity of the fact is that I am a native of Windia, Quinea Konary. But I fell in love with Manankasidou and Njawara village. I am happy at my work at the Gambia General Hospital, Manding Medical Centre at Njawara. But it goes deeper than that for Njawara is the trading Centre and gateway between Gambia and neighboring Republic of Senegal. This village is unique because of its neighborliness and friendliness and community spirit usually associated with villagers. In Banjul, I always felt like an insignificant person, and the patients I cared were nothing more than cases. Here at Njawara, I found villagers looked upon nurses as friends, and often, after they are better, they invited nurses to their homes for dinner or some family celebration. This allows nurses bonding with the community and felt liked or loved as well as being helpful to a person(s)."

On the next day Kunsa Mori told his elder brother Oustas Mori his intention about Majula Seyabalo. Oustas Mori could not fathom the fact that kunsa had his eyes set on a woman. Kunsa who since high school had no interest or time for girls was now enamored. Hence Oustas Mori was more than eager to meet the devil girl who swooned his brother. He begged Kunsa to let him come and meet this phantom. He wondered what spells she caste on poor Kunsa his younger brother. Oustas told the family and the lonely dissenter was their only sister Jainaba who thought Kunsa was impotent from the word go and that the girl might be taking advantage of him because of his prospects of soon becoming a medical doctor. Asked why she replied, "I felt that way". She told the family "I had pushed all sorts of girls onto my brother but he rebuffed all unabashed. Hence I hatched a conspiracy surprised visit unannounced to Kunsa and Majula Seyabalo".

Kunsa mean while out of share joy that he made the right choice of a woman informed his family, friends and closed professors at the medical school. His friends were more than elated and planned a party for the Easter brake in honor of Kunsa Mori and Fatou. Knusa and Majula Seyabalo soon to be couples were very happy to have such loyal fund loving friends. They looked forward to the party with exuberance.

On the following Saturday, the surprised visitors rang Kuna's door bell at 5 pm. He was so surprised at first that he thought that something serious most have taken place but soon he tamed his nerves and ushered them into the flat with an apology in the way books were thrown all over the floor and tables. There was a skeleton sitting on one of the chairs because Kunsa was reviewing his Anatomy lessons at the time of their arrival. The family told of their delight in the good news of him having a girl he considers seriously and they came to have it confirmed by him. Kunsa Mori gleefully told his family, "I have finally met a lady of my heart and she was true love made for me. She and said I literally agreed on every aspect of life, goal and faith". His father like Jainaba was not convinced and jokingly said, "Old boy show us the Madonna of your heart. We are dying to meet our daughter in-law." Kunsa smiled knowing his father and only sister would be the last converts to accepting that he was a normal male but had no incentive for girls until the moment and day he met Majula Seyabalo. He picked up the phone and gave a quick dial and soon a voice came on the loud speaker. Majula Seyabalo said "Hello darling. I am in the shower. I will call back soon in five minutes. Is everything ok with you and are you studying?"

Both parents were struck by this genuine concern for their son from the lady he loved and they from that moment liked her already not even having seen her in person. Their son has finally found a good mate. However skeptical Jainaba still held onto her ground until more proof comes from the lady in question. Not long Majula Seyabalo rang and apologized but was now on the way. Kunsa said smilingly, "Darling my parents are here to meet you". "I will be right there retorted the melodious voice". Kunsa looked with a broad smile on his face as if telling his siblings to eat their hearts out for he has Majula Seyabalo for good. A taxi stopped by and out came the most beautiful lady in the block and a radiant lady stepped towards Kunsa's flat. She rang the bell, curtseyed and hugged Kunsa as soon as the door was let ajar. He held her and they walked hand in hand to the center of the room before the awaiting guests. Oustas Mori was petrified by her beauty and good manners and tipped his hat off unaware. His father was wide mouthed and Jainaba was dying of admiration of the sphinx before them. To skeptical Jainaba Majula Seyabalo turned out to be perfection and beauty rolled in one mould. She was natural and had neither mascara nor false eyelashes on.

Alas the family finally welcomed Majula into their hearts for the jewel she was and joy she brought them in loving Kunsa Mori. They instantly assured her of their love and support for her and Kunsa. Majula graciously said, "thank you and I promise to be a worthy member of the family". The statement took Kunsa by surprise, as it seems to push things advancing. The entourage decided to have a lunch at a nearby restaurant. Again Majula proved superb by refusing offers of alcohol beverages or cigarettes from friends of her would be father in-law. Instead her effect on the father in-law was so profound that he binned the last cigarettes he was smoking and vowed not to smoke for the rest of his live. His wife was delighted that Majula had such promising effect on her stubborn husband whom she had been trying to persuade from smoking and to moderate his alcohol intake. They enjoyed the rest of the day over meals and soft drinks and reminiscence of their own high school days. It was all a dream come true for the family and especially for Kunsa Mori who finally made the right decision of having select the best mate. The day went well and the family drove home leaving Kunsa Mori and Majula lapsed back to their daily schedules and promises. Majul was so elated about meeting Kunsa's family that she called her parents and friends and told them the miracle man she met recently.

Her parents were more than delighted for her and the good news she conveyed. In the mean time Kunsa and Fatou kept their promise of not disturbing each during weekdays and exam times. If they venture to text it has to be during long breaks or lunchtime. Both did well at their exams before the Easter holidays. They later during the brake attended what turned out to be the most enjoyable and memorable dream party friends ever threw in behaves of Kunsa and Majula. All their friends and mostly Kunsa's high school and college classmates attended the gala occasion of the Easter break. The music of the night ranged from current to ancient classical Greek, Roman, Africa, Reggae, and Latin America tunes. Majula had deep appreciation and saw herself fortunate to be in love and loved by Kunsa Mori. The music stopped at the stroke of midnight and Kunsa was asked to say something to Majula. While he was searching and trying to get a word or two out a friend pushed a golden ring studded with the highest quality diamonds into his hand. This was a great moment for Kunsa and dream come true and he took the great leap of his life and pulled the surprise of the night. Hence he cleared his throat amid dead silence of a parked hall and said, "Ladies and gentlemen, Majula Seyabalo and I express profound gratitude for your being true friends and by what you have done to make us happy.

It is a true mark of friendship. He then spontaneously moved toward Majula, knelt facing her and gently held her hand, looked straight into eyes and blushing face, placed the ring in hand and said Majula, "I am fondly in love with you, I love you and want you to marry me. It will give me profound pleasure to be your husband". Majula, in shock and unable to control tears of joy replied, "I love you too and would be exceptionally happy to belong to you and be bearer of you children. I promise to be your wife during better and hard or difficult and worse times in our lives." Kunsa nervously placed the engagement ring into her ring finger and they embraced and kissed fervently among the loudest cheers and blaring music and to envy of most of the girls in the crowd. Both had no doubts that their parents would welcome this night as another memorable step in their own lives. The night ended late in the wee hours as it herald in the engagement of a pseudo prince and princess in love. All the tabloid papers in the following day had this story as headline news of love made in heaven. Verses of the event intermingled with pictures and commentary from friends about these two enamored lovers filled papers for three publications.With everyone gone the engaged, Kunsa and Majula reflected on the evening and what it meant for their lives.

Kunsa more than any reflected on the new roll and responsibility and impact it will have on his medical career. He had no doubts of having made the right decision for he adores this lady that embraced his heart. He promised himself to make her the happiest wife on planet earth. He called his parents as well as the in-laws and told them that the wedding will take place after both graduated from their various colleges. Mean while Kunsa and Majula became instant celebrities in Njawara, their city and friends as well as unknown people or tourist to the place asked for their autographs or to singe over their pictures cut from journals. The media continue to compete as which one will be the first to break news of the great wedding day. They bribed, placed interview request to the families of both lovers and even made up their own astrological calendars for it. They dwelt on the possible quality of the wedding dress and where the couple plans to take their honeymoon. So-called friends and classmates were paid to be moles to extract the above from either party. All these media frenzy and side-winding methods failed to have Kunsa and Majula fall for traps the media set and it made them even more popular as lot more was written about the would be fairy tale wedding of the year for the city. All of which brought great sales to these daily papers.

While the media busied itself on selling tips about the couple's plans, Kunsa and Majula continued on their studies and visiting relatives. The media hipped these visits and created lots of unknown uncles, aunts, friends and x-lovers of these would soon be couples. Yes, some jealous girls had daring minds to accept money and allow their names connect to such ridiculous unfounded fabrications to fan public consumption of the tabloids. The following week Kunsa and Majula drove to the home of their in-laws some five hours drive away. The moment they took onto the Highway a fleet of paparazzi photographers vying to get the best shots as they followed causing an unexpected chase amidst flash photography of every move the couple did. At Banjul, the couples were surprised by an even bigger audience and were showered with gifts from family members, friends and the public. Again the media hipped every event of the coming or would be the big social event of the year at Njawara while Kunsa and Majula tried to adjust to the new reality of their current lives. Congratulatory notes, cards and letters poured in from all corners of the city and provinces honoring their decision to be married. Kuusa being a shy-man and less than a social event addict never liked the limelight he found himself and suffered the most from questioners and media.

He thought his life was private affair until this day when it became an open book to the public. Thanks to media hypes. Both Majula and Kunsa managed to cope with the intrusion but stuck to their plan of not telling anything about the wedding until the appropriate time. This left the media doing what it was best at, guessing and creating attractive stories to keep sales up and interest of its readers afire. Amidst the above helter skelter Kunsa managed to graduate from medical school and was offered residency program after completing his internship at Gambia General teaching hospital. Majula Seyabalo had also sailed through her State Registered Nursing program and was also doing specialize nursing training at the same hospital before they finally proceed to the self-help village health medical center at Kerr Bahen. This achieved the couple now turned onto their plans for the future and their pending wedding.

Dr. Alhasan Sisawo Ceesay, MD

Chapter 4

TURNING INTO NEW LEAF

The heat turned onto Chaga Musu, nick named, Tulunna Jenela Sile, hurting her feelings and rights she believed sacrosanct to all humans. The news did not go down well for Majula Seyabalo's younger cousin, Chaga Musu Tulunna. She lived a swinger's life leaving the community wishing that she changed her life style of the past thirty - four years. She dropped out of high school and took off with a sailor to France where she stayed for ten years before returning to Africa.

She now works at an All in one Indian take away restaurant for the past three years. Her numerous male friends, namely Abdurahim Jalo, Monkey face Jalo, Abdu Bastra, Malibali Dannsu, Gujo Sower, Samba Sung, Malibali Wages, Mbower, Amata ,,wasar Malibali and Ebuse Wutusung are known to be involved in drugs trafficking, pimping, and alcohol, which made it hard for ordinary village men to ask her hand in marriage. The saying, "tell me who your friends are and I can almost tell your character," holds true for this young lady. She still moves with seven other girls who styled themselves as the Swinging Cooperasey.

Some armchair psychiatrist had already termed pretty
Chaga Musu Tulunna a borderline disturbed personality
and her parents did once apply their own psychological
studies to her case. Hold your guns for Musu did an
unexpected u-turn upon returning from two years wild
tour of England, Australia and New Zealand. Let no one
fool you Chaga Musu was a beauty in her own right and
very likable lady. This awareness led her to lose control of
herself and moved with some wrong women groups.
Chaga Musu is brilliant but high school bored her and
that lead to her looking outward for more challenging
things of life. She taught herself mathematics, chemistry
and physics but hated the classroom structure and her
parents were too poor to enroll a private tutoring for her.
In contrast to Majula Musu loves life and swinging night
clubs Tell you how good she was at certain time, is that
she used to help Majula with her homework in the core
sciences. On arrival, she rushed to hug her cousin whom
she missed a lot and last but not the least Chaga Musu
rushed to Kunsa Mori and knelt to congratulate them and
told how she got the news from as far away as New
Zealand. She presented both presents from friends Down
under. It was a kind gesture that went well and signaling
change in the street girl's attitude.

She learned a lot about mixing and making friends on cruises and at beaches all over tourist Mecca she visited. Chaga Musu also had a great surprise lined up for the family and eager media. She let a broad smile and revealed, "I happy to let all know that a rich multimillionaire Italian, who would be visiting next week, had spoken or asked for my hand in marriage". At first no one paid attention to her believing that Chaga Musu was up to one of her numerous antiques. Knowing the surprise in store for the skeptic she bid them goodnight and went to bed straight for she still suffered from jet lack after a long hull from Down under. Kunsa, again thanked everyone for the presents and for coming to enjoy and celebrate the moment. The media tried all it could to extract the date for the wedding and failed. Lot of the guests left by 8 pm leaving Kunsa, Majula, and his in-laws at home. It was decided to have dinner at nearby hotel amour, only finding them being surrounded by waiting paparazzi and media. Kunsa and Majula descended from their car and rushed, amidst questions and flash photography, into the restaurant and headed for a special VIP dinning room at the second floor. This way the restaurant owner thought or hoped only close family and friends could attend and have a peaceful meal. Was it to be so ordained?

No, the media had other ideas for they and the paparazzi decided to use cranes and ladders to position themselves near windows for a snap shot of the dinner couple which photos will fetch them hundreds if not millions of dollars. Kunsa had to beg Majula not to mind but go on doing what she wished. Majula in a whisper told Kunsa, "One can now imagine what pain Diana; Princess of Wales, had to endure from minute by minute hounding paparazzi in the name of photographic journalism". The dinner went well despite such pressures from news and photo seekers. Kunsa and Majula had to use the train for their return journey to Njawara unknown to the media, which planned to escort the latter for a while in the hope of getting more photos of the couple kissing or holding hands. Even Oustas Mori, Kunsa's brother at Njawara, found himself cornered by the paparazzi. They attempted to give him a camera for the provision of photos of the couple and in return they were going to pay him a hefty sum. Oustas although needed money at the time was not going to betray his brother for gold or pennies. Hence he refused the offer and asked them out of his home without a second thought about it. This act not only cemented him more with his brother but it earned him respect, trust and love from Majula Seyabalo.

Oustas' wife Bintou Hadume was furious at him for not taking the money, which would have enable her buy a dress she saw at the high street shop. Oustas told her "I will not sell my brother's blood nor was I going to be part of the destruction of this dream love made in heaven. He said, "Let us leave that which the Gods anointed to the Gods. No one has right to set it asunder because of selfishness and jealousy. I love you and will do every thing for you but that excludes being a pirate on my family especially my blood brother." Mean while Chaga Musu Tulunna woke up from her stupor with a mighty hang over. Monday, to everyone's surprise Chaga Musu decided to have a family meeting. She started by telling the family, "I apologizing for all my bad behaviors that were going on for too long. I assure you that I from today severed my relation with the Swinging Cooperaseyn and that above all, whether you believed me or not, I will never drink alcohol or take drugs again for the rest of my life."Everyone in the room drew a shy of relief for some reason they believed her now without much reason for it. It was just the way she delivered and touched their hearts by the candor of her intentions. They prayed it stays so for her own shake as age is catching up with her not being married. They concluded that it was high time she got out of the high school free for all life style she lead for too long a time.

The last surprising announcement from Chaga Musu was that her millionaire Italian lover called last night and was due on Friday. She assured everyone one that this tycoon neither drinks alcohol nor takes drugs but strictly a business oriented gentleman. A few skeptics thought she was hallucinating for a habit carried on as long as she did was hard to break away. Well brace up readers for this family has turned to be one of the most fortunate as Chaga Musu Tulunna set Njawara into Alice in wonderland fairy tale story. The mare fact Chaga Musu was now free of drugs and all her colorful habit was miracle in itself. It was transformation and a good example for despondent youth to follow and be free of drugs. Every one held their breath for Friday, the day of the Italian tycoon as some mockingly doped. Helicopter pad had already been prepared and ceremonies arranged to welcome the guest. Thursday saw the arrival of the media who poured in their drones. Business was brisk and vendors from all over poured into Njawara to share the blessing Chaga Musu Tulunna rained onto the region. She has reformed from the repugnant society hated to one adored by it with scribes and poets writing about her. She and Njawara were now poised and eager to meet her lover from Italy in less than twenty hours.

Friday arrived with clear blue skies and Njawara was brought to life when they notice the arriving helicopter drowned the city. A long queue of black limos plied through the street heading to 222 Love Lane Street in Njawara. Mean while the Helicopter circle the city several times while boxes upon boxes of presents were offloaded from the limos in front of 222 Love lanes Street, the home of gorgeous Chaga Musu Tulunna. Soon the helicopter landed gently and out came a young handsome gentleman dressed in the most elegant three-piece business suit accompanied by the pilot. Musu Tulunna was at this time at the doors of 222 Love lanes joyfully waiting to meet her knight of the day. She came out when she heard people saying it was all like a dream that Chaga Musu would be this transformed and blessed with such fabulous luck. She walked out of the house and by the time she reached halfway to the lead limo the Italian tycoon ran towards her. The media and paparazzi went into frenzy in an effort to record every minute of the exciting unfolding history of Chaga Musu' life. Villagers were wide-eyed and just happy to witness a miracle unfolding before their very eyes. The gentleman, in real Italian fashion, picked Chaga Musu Tulunna off her feet, kissed her, while heading to the house. He was very pleased to note change in her domino. He loved her very much and feels lifted having her in his hands.

He promised to never to let her stray away from him for the rest of their lives. Throngs of admirers and news media followed flabbergasted by romance never ever seen in Njawara. He set her down at the door and embraced every family member as if he had known him or her for ages. He just blended without the air of importance some other rich fellow treats peasants like the villagers he was among. He was an instant hit with the folks and drums, dancing and songs from villagers vibrated in melody never heard or witnessed in the region. People went wild when he asked for one of the boxes to be opened and money given to the people. He ordered slaughter of three five-year-old bulls for the villagers to feast upon. The news made people fifty miles away to rush to witness phenomenon of the year. It was a rare field day for the media and paparazzi as some filled the city with rumors that Chaga Musu Tulluna had landed a Mafioso man from Italy who might rejuvenate Njawara. In reality Alexandro was neither a Mafioso nor a drug dealer as alleged by jealous people. Njawara will never be the tranquil village it was for Musu's transformation has swept it along. Alexandro was a clean businessman who made a covenant never to raise money by means of drug market, prostitutes or Mafioso route.

Back at Love lane Alexandro invited Chaga Musu, her family and friends to join him at one of the VIP service four-star hotels in the city. The trip to the hotel with Chaga Musu Tulunna seated at the back side by side to her lover was more than fairy tale. It was a Hollywood atmosphere all day.

At the hotel and after a king's feast Alexandro pulled out an engagement ring and necklace and knelt, with the crowd aghast, asked Chaga Musu Tulunna to be his wife. This shocked Musu Tulluna who was not expecting that to happen so soon. She was promised a surprise but not this momentous in her life. Chaga Musu Tulunna fainted briefly but picked up her composer and said, "Yes, I love you and it's a privilege to be your loving wife and mother of your children". He placed the engagement ring and hugged and kissed her several times amides cheers from onlookers and media.

The applauding went on almost for half an hour before waning. Mean while, the fairy tale couple charmed everyone with smiles and kissed over and over to the pleasure of the crowd.The Njawara phenomenon became headline in all the major newspapers of the day and Chaga Musu and Alexandro's photos were displayed in nearly all the papers and some requested advert contract with pretty Chaga Musu Tulunna.

What did Njawara gained from this union? First, Alexandro contracted for the modest home of Chaga Musu's parents to be brought to modern standards with forty-bedroom facility before his return in three months time. He paid the cost to build such edifice right then and there and work began the moment he left for Italy. In addition he donated two million Euros for the village to build a school and repair some of the roads leading to it. A permanent helicopter pad was also built. Soon business rushed to Njawara and people once again had hopes of employment and life to look forward to. Thanks to Chaga Musu Tulunnna's transformation. For weeks this fairy tale engagement became not only the talk of the town but headlines all over the regional papers. Musu's popularity soared for few women sober or not were able to bring such luck and status as happened. Musicians rushed to cut records with lyrics about Chaga Musu and Alexandro. The family took the whole development with stride and caution because they were still in denial of the gift brought to them by Chaga Musu Tulunna's change for a better life. It was like a dream and they fear to wake up and find themselves at lower level than they were before Alexandro. Alexandro had planned this trip to be a get to know Chaga Musu's family and he had to return the next day.

At the helicopter pad, the couple kissed and kissed as if the world was about to end or that it was the last time they will see each other alive. Finally the handsome Italian got onboard the helicopter and soared high in the sky with his hand still out waving good-bye to Chaga Musu Tulunna. Chaga Musu rejoined her family and thanked them and again apologized for her previous street life. Some started contemplating what type of wedding this would be and where it would be held. Others were brave enough to believe it will be held in an Old Italian castle with only family and friends allowed to attend. Like Kunsa Mori and Majula Seyabalo their wedding plans was kept as top secret. Majula and Musu had agreed to have their wedding on the same day and place not to be undisclosed until three weeks to the actual event. The family remained tight lipped and dignified than bloating about the luck of their daughters. This made the media nervous and anxious to gain control of the events as they unfold. Hence they again, like in Kunsa's engagement, went into a frenzy of leaking half-truths and presenting interviews with retired teachers claiming to have taught the couple at various levels of schooling. This was done to outwit and sell more than their competitors. The media even allowed speculation that the couple will be wedded in London or Italy instead of the Gambia.

Thank God both the medical college and nursing school band granting interviews from the media for fear of disruption of lessons. Alexandro and entourage left days ago and will not be back to Njawara for three or five months. Kunsa and Majula were very happy for Chaga Musu and Alexandro's engagement. They sent presents and wished the couple a very successful and happy fruitful relationship. They promised to do all they could to help propel this gift Musu landed. Musu and Majula paid several secrete visits to Alexandro in Italy and both came to like Alexandro the tycoon for the simple amiable person he was. Above all they respected his business skills and magnificent way he disarms his competitors. The two ladies loved Monica, Alexandro's sister. Monica was all smiles and gave them a warm welcome to the castle Alexandro and his parents leaved. His mother was frail and in the late eighties but was alert and cheerful like all Italians normally are with visitor. She hugged her daughter in-law Chaga Musu Tulunna and gave several kisses on her cheeks. The home was the epitome or zenith and trappings of wealth. This castle was one of several Alexandro owns in Italy. He had few villas built in Kenya, India, Nigeria and even Senegal of all places. He owns two helicopters, specially built luxury yachters and one of kind cruise liners. Asked why the cruise liners. He replied, "To rest comfortable on the sea."

Chaga Musu and Majula were flabbergasted by such display of wealth and luxury. Chaga Musu could hardly believe that that was going to be her empire and that all she had to do was to wish or ask and it shall be delivered on a golden platter. On this visit they had their dinner on board one of the luxury liners at the middle of the Caribbean Sea. This ship was on the same day renamed Chaga Musu's Paradise. All was set and blue-sky, moon and stars lit the way. The candle light dinner tables befit royalty and not for simple peasant girls like Chaga Musu and Majula. Alexandro, the girls and invited friends ate and enjoyed music all the evening and then everyone retired to their luxurious cabins. The girls hard arranged to sleep in the same cabin to keep promise of not being intimate with their future husbands until the day of their honeymoon. Strange enough but this was how conservative and self-disciplined girls were in Chaga Musu and Majula's days. Yes, women jealously guarded their dignity until the right moment comes instead of falling for today's common one-night standers. The cruiser sailed back to port and the girls clandestinely left for the Gambia after being spoiled by lavish gifts from Alexandro and friends.

Chapter 5

A SECRET WEDDING PLAN

Legend has it that Chaga Musu and Majula Seyabalo, with blessings of their husbands to be, had agreed for the weddings to take place in three months time at the grand love hotel in Njawara the Gambia. This they kept the most guarded secret from friends and media. In the interim the girls felt like being in dreamland and hoped they wake with stars and the situation still real for them. They supported and encourage each other during the preparation for the grandest occasion and cerebration of the region. They avoided straying and from believing rumors from media gimmickry. They promised to make the men who touched their hearts with love and help to shape their future happy. Majula reminded Chaga Musu that she and Kunsa Mori, in response to their call, would be manning a self-help village health medical center further down in the provinces but distance will not separate them. Perhaps Alexandro will visit the center sooner than later after the wedding. Majula said to Musu, "We assure you (Musu) of our continued love and willingness to offer guidance any time you and Alexandro needed it. With misty eyes Chaga Musu apologized for all the bad things she had been to the family and friends.

The two affirm their love for each other and hugged for ten minutes in-between sobs. The tick of the old grandfather's clock was the only sound heard while the girls went into a silent prayer for their future. At this hour the well-meaning angel in both girls surfaced. The moment was so touching that only the heartless would remain unmoved. They got up and walked hand in hand towards Alexandro who did not disturb their solace. He smilingly held Chaga Musu and said, "Darling it is time for your being away for a few more weeks and assured her that his life is woven around her's." On their way and on-board the special made private jet to UK, the girls reminiscent on their Italian experience. Chaga Musu secretly pinched herself to be certain that she was in a real private jet flying over countries transporting none but just the two of them and flight crew. The luxury in the jet was beyond heir imagination. Never in their early life, whether in primary or high school life, did it occur to them that life would be this kind to them after college. Yes, boys at one time or the other have made appreciable remarks about perfection and beauty of their features and facial presentation. Some admirers even dared to compare them with Rachael Welch and Marling Monroe of America.

However, the girls now swore to use their newfound gift to be role models by displaying acceptable social attitudes and contributing positively to community they may find themselves. Chaga Musu promised to set up a charity to help hungry people and drug addicts. Majula had already committed herself to helping Kunsa's self-help village health project flourish. They are doing this with intense believe that they are their community's keeper and that the good we do on earth should not be buried or interred with our bones but should out live us for the benefit of generations to follow. They asked, "what was the use of money if one hoards it and turned a miser while others live in deprivation and hunger of no fault of theirs? No, not creating free loafers but giving a helping hand to raise both spirit and efforts of the downtrodden to rise to better levels in this life. All able bodies should be able to work for descent life of their own and not be saddled under cloaks of ingenious welfare systems that only make them poorer in their self worth and income." Alexandro had since twelve years ago opened business in Kenya, Senegal and Egypt in Africa with similar goal in mind. Now well over five thousand families benefit from his African enterprises. He once told Chaga Musu that with her on his side they could guarantee help for even more poor villagers in Africa and the developing world.

All of which is predicated on Chaga Musu having thrown her frivolous life with a change to a new leaf for everyone's benefit. Chaga Musu affirmed and said, "I am a brand new born again lady and my old ways are in the past for good because I wanted to be loved and to belong to a good thing in this life". Alexandro and Chaga Musu were happy that their lives were cemented not only for themselves but to be charitable to the needy. With the above desire to turn into a new leaf in their minds the girls started to seriously reflect on when and where to be wedded. As expected many publications about the girls and their future husbands filled bookshops and daily tabloids. It spoke of solidarity between the families, the girls, and their finances. The girls landed back home at midnight and drove quietly home without the paparazzi getting a field day to feed the media frenzy. Needless to say, their lives never returned to tranquility as the media scrutinizes their behaviors, dress and manner of speech. Princess Diana would have been in total empathy with the girls for lack of privacy they are under going from the hands of media and paparazzi. They can now see how there was no freedom, human rights or even law for respect of the individual's right to be free of press harassment.Everyone, especially the press, wanted to make money off them and had daring minds to style them celebrity only because of the promised wealth combined with facial beauty. Young girls are encouraged to be copycats, when their parents knew that the poor things would never look like Chaga Musu and Majula Seyabalo or the luck that surfaced for them. Some called the paparazzi cameramen hooligans because of the deliberate ways they brandish cameras onto faces not resonating with such a wish or expectation of those being photographed.

Front: Fatou Dibba and Isatou Dibba

Back: Dr. Ceesay, Mrs. Famatanding Tarawale holding Penda Dibba, and Babucarr Dibba

Media frenzy now turned Njawara and the entire region into state of primigravida society in painful gestation in expectancy of the region's biggest event. Aching for the mother of all weddings everyone wondered where it would take place, whether the weddings were going to be separate and who would be on the official invitation list of that historic day of days for the region.

No one knew details of the wedding because the couples wanted to complete their academic and professional career preparations before letting the cat out of the bag. Time has now allowed Chaga- Musu to mature and grow beyond wildest expectations. She now acts maturely and is confident of herself.

The plans were finally consummated at a family meeting held secretly in Italy away from the Paparazzi and media. There the future couples agreed that the wedding would happen jointly at the great hall of lovers in Njawara, the Gambia. The occasion will be an interfaith officiating and all major religions will be represented and will offer prayers. It was agreed that the wedding take place on the first Friday after harvest to enable all villagers wanting to participate in the ceremony attend. A list of who is who not only in the Badibous but also in the political arena was wisely drawn from spectrum of politicians.

The media started vying for locations and people to interview on the great day even though it would be three months before the girls take their vows. The tabloids and various village organizations went into frenzy of preparation as to who would be most artistic and perform the most remembered feat of all dances. Neighboring villages in Senegal cashed in and prepared to take the show on the day of days for the region. The city of Njawara is an old colonial trading center and gateway to the northern region of the Republic of Senegal. It lies on the grassy banks of the Miniminiyang bolong, a creek of the River Gambia, in the North Bank Region. Mandinka, Wolof, Serere and a few Jolas inhabit Njawara city. In this fringes of the Gambia will soon take place the region's most historic even after the Saitmatie crusade in the 1920s. Both Majula Seyabalo and Chaga Musu are members of the Mandinka tribe whose great grandparents migrated from now Republic of Mali to the Badibous in the Gambia. The girls were groomed, like their parents before them, to become good farmers and house wives. Their great, great, grandparents, unlike the break homes these girls live in, lived in huts and mud houses some distance away from the fields.Njawara was then a rural village with few thousand inhabitants with no roads, only bush paths through thick savanna grass.

It had an abundance of cattle, horses, goats and sheep grazing in the vacant fields. Hence Njawara has metamorphosized into the metropolitan city you are about to celebrate history of a magnificent twin wedding. The momentousness of the occasion left Majula Seyabalo and Chaga Musu at lost in the welter of thousand details. Every aspect was well orchestrated and their wedding dresses looked superb and admirable. Alexandra gladly paid for the bills and more. All was set by midday of Thursday twenty fours to wedding day. Young ladies in towns and villages wished their day to be half as historic and romantic as the one they are about to witness. Soon the Alice in wonderland wedding of princes and princess dawned. Mean while Njawara swelled to almost quarter of a million by the last week of the month of the wedding. Buntings and flags flew all over the city as if it were going to have a coronation. The Lovers' hall at Hotel De amour had a special facelift and a makeover with effigies of the ladies and their feature husbands on display. Security was beefed up well in advance of the ceremony for fear of trouble from competitors. Friday, the day of the wedding, dawned bright and clear. Njawara was turned into the largest gathering of happy, cheering, smiling, dancing villagers, and onlookers lining the streets to have a glimpse of the cars of the brides and bridegrooms.

People in celebrant mood struggled with flags, buntings in hand to see the bridal cars. It was not until after midday that the procession to Hotel de amour began with people cheering, throwing rice, flowers and even kisses at the bridal cars. The bridal cars crawled to a standstill because of people eager or wanting to touch them or place their bouquet of flowers on them. Finally the bridal entourage reached the hall and proud and happy fathers of the ladies met them at the door and walked the isles to hand them over to take their vows gracefully. Fatou and Musu were just radiant and charming to behold. On this lovely Friday Majula Seyabalo and Chaga Musu took their vows to be wedded to their respective husbands. This was good omen for villagers who just had a bumper harvest added to this once in a life ceremony in behalf of one their own. The ceremony officiated by priests from all major denominations took full two hours before the married couples could stand at a special balcony erected for the purpose to thank those who in any way made it so warm and historic for them and Njawara. They then joined VIPs and invited guests at the banquet hall for the reception. From this formal reception the couples headed to the square at the center of the city, where the scene looked like a great sea of villagers, to witness the most colorful display of dance, acrobats, wrestling, and spectacular feat of magic performed by various groups and villages. Yes, events of the wedding ceremony reverberated in every village and hamlet of the Badibous. The television, media and paparazzi had a field day and many people vied to be interviewed or photographed while hold pictures of the wedded. Kunsa and Alexandro jointly provide all the food, a dozen bulls were slaughter for the villagers to feast on. The celebrations continued to the wee hours of the night before the people went to rest. It picked from where it ended on Friday right through Wednesday before the celebrants called it quit. Njawara was overwhelmed with the sense of history and joy this wedding brought to it. The city will never be the same again for it will now be inundated with more tourists than it ever dreamt of. Mean while the married couple had left quietly to one of Alexandro's luxury liners to spend their honeymoons at the Caribbean Sea. They returned two weeks later with Chaga Musu and Alexandro heading to Milan in Italy. Majula Seyabalo and Kunsa Morri headed to their village Medical Center in response to their call. Chaga Musu continued to surprise people by nurturing her transformation by volunteering to help the elderly and at the same time she set up a treatment center for drug addicts and orphans at Kerewan village a stone throw away from Njawara.

Njawara Babti Yassin

The in-laws shuttled between Njawara and Milan to visit Alexandro and Chaga Musu. Alexandro continued to give lavish presents of dresses, gold necklaces, and sailing trips aboard his luxury cruiser. Alexandro and Chaga Musu paid a surprise visit to Njawara and in particular to Majula and Kunsa Morri at their village health NGO. Alexandro wondered what the former colonial rulers did for the poor of the Gambia if such basic things like hospitals, good drinking water, schools, farming, and electricity hardly existed in these villages after three hundred plus years of ruling the country. The most generous of Alexandro' contribution was helping Majula and Kunsa set up the children's hospital of their medical center. He also provided scholarships and grants for those wishing to become nurses and doctors serving the center. Such benevolence and success at his business propelled Alexandro to the envy of the Mafia, the most heinous group in Italy. Soon he found dead fish thrown at his door with little threatening notes attached. The most serious requested him to hand over all his assets and businesses to the almighty Mafioso or he and his family would face severe retributions. Alexandro reporting this to the police accelerated action from the Mafia. They burnt one villa he loves most to the ground and killed an uncle.

This prompted Alexandro to yield to their command and found his way to America under different pseudonyms. Meanwhile Musu Jenela returned to the Gambia and stayed with her family. The change in fortune of Alexandro and the fact that time and distance can make the heart fonder she started showing signs of breaking down. It is said that one cannot separate the leopard from it spots nor can we teach an old dog new tricks. This applied to Musu Jenela as she reverted to the street concealed at first and later doing it openly. Yes, this village girl, floozy Musu Jenela, thought her wiser than all around and that she could place woolen veils on the faces of the community while doing her dirty actions. She got so shameless and nonchalant about her uncouth behaviors that one day she took all three children of Alexndro with her to her boy friend. When Alexandro learnt about it and asked her why she did such dirty game to him. She replied by asking if she had no right to get male friends. That infuriated Alexandro but being in America he had to cool off and sort help by asking friends and those in the know to look into the story before he takes drastic action. Musu Jenela got worse in the end. She allowed endless chain of lovers to sleep in while Alexandro's children are around. Her dranged if not tangled mind lead her into bringing her sex partner, monkey face Jalongor, to sleep with her while the children were in their rooms. Lo and behold both she and monkey face miss calculated the suspicion of the children who pretended to be asleep when the two arrived at the house. Musu Jenela even counter checked to be certain they were asleep. Not too long the children, while peeping from their door, saw this shameless ad ultra, monkey face, crawl into their mother's room. The children wanted to call the police but could not because they accidentally left their mobiles at their mother's bedroom. Monkey face had a getaway car parked just two hundred yards from the main gate in the event things got wrong he could escape in seconds from the scenery. Musu Jenela and monkey face got up 5:30 am and had the nerves to kiss their dirty goodbyes at the center of the yard before full gaze of the children, thinking them asleep. It got so bad that the elder child called Musu Jenela and placed an ultimatum that next time her lovers sleep in the house she and her sister will run away and never to come back or accept her as their mother. Musu grew to be an embarrassment to not only the children but also all Alexandro's relatives and friends. In the end none associated with her. She remained aloof as if though in manic denial. Being very comfortable in the villa Alexandro built for her in Gambia and he being in America afforded her loose opportunity to regress and revert to her old bad ways i.e. the street, men, and drugs with phi nest. She stooped so low that adultery became a regular high way for her and her male partner monkey face Jalongor. This left Alexandro depressed for months on end because Musu Jenela had before their engagement promised never to be a street or gruna-girl for the rest of her life should he marry her.

Concerned friends bombarded Alexandro with sad escapees of Musu Jenela. This, Alexandro made known to Musu Jenela but was not tempted to devoice her yet because of his love for her and the children they had in the good days. He never wanted to see his children yarning for a mother or a father.

He wants to keep the family unit under one roof and not a separated one where the children will be torned between the parents. Besides, he loved this lady with every sinew and heart he had and could not recon this beast in a woman's body was what he married. Her acts were so shameful and degrading that he thought a curse must have been cast upon him for leasing his life to such a degrading monster of a prostitute.

This once esteemed lady has now turned into an offensive tart and a slut of the highest category and still believes she could fool people into not noticing or seeing through her filthy life.

The threat from the children only made her switch rendezvous zones knowing that the children in a telephone conversation to their dad confirmed their intentions to run away should their mother continue to act so disgracefully and pain it were causing them. Alexandro was so shocked that he called cousin-blest heart Ayata to look into the allegation coming from his children.

From that day he channeled the children's allowance through cousin Ayata at the same time he confronted Musu Jenela about the heart wrenching shameless acts. All Musu Jenela could or was able to say in her defense was she had nothing to say. This alone was a hallmark of guilt. She later threatened the kids to cause the elder one to go to cousin Ayata for few hours to sought solace from the embarrassment.

The straw that almost broke gentle and kind Alexandro's back and let pure love sink in the sea of desperation was the deepest and most personal, if not bizarre, experience he and the children ever had to endure. Lasting characteristics makes us who we are and for Musu Jebela it portrays self-deprecation to say the least.

Dr. Alhasan Sisawo Ceesay, MD

Nurse Majula, a cousin of Musu, tried all she could by counseling and advising the family to take Musu Jenela for expert psychiatric and medical evaluation before things get out of hand further. Musu Jenela, in her illusionary, deluded and hallucinatory mine, believes she was maligned by those who wanted money from her. She was just having a good time before her beloved husband returns from America. Her social imbalance seems to be a curse pushing her into earthly hell. Loosing Alexandro and the kids would tantamount to irretrievable loss indeed. Some dare think that her current behaviors may be due to cognitive impairment. Alexandro also held such slim spider's web believe in this likelihood that he vowed not to devoice her while looking for possible cure or psychiatric intervention that could save his lover. Musu Jenela provided pseudo-psychiatrists a field day of speculations and unfounded conclusions as to why this regression in Musu Jenela's life. They labeled her current setback as psychotic and hyperactive sex phenomenon. They dared to recommend both cognitive and behavioral therapy in conjunction with local witchcraft approaches. One beguiles the truth by saying that every thing about Musu Jenela pointed toward a decompensated end-stage of the most romantic affair that ever happened at Njawara.

Legend has it that Alexandro had to come to the Gambia take Musu and the children to America where he sought treatment for her. A miracle never ceases to happen or failed Musu Jenela who suddenly recovered and became a shy caring mother. She comfiest of not being aware of the childish and disgraceful acts she was alleged to have been committing. To cut a long story, Alexandro being a fighter, completed his law degree at Boston University and established a very big law firm while Musu Jenela enrolled in computer science course with a major in mathematics at a college nearby. She graduated magna cum lauded and is now teaching at a junior college with intention of doing a masters degree in science and becoming a professor one fine day. Only pure and unadulterated love glued Alexandro to Chaga Musu, alias Musu Jenela. As for Majula Seyabalo and Kunsa Mori, the call of establishing a medical center to provide medical aid to villagers went exceptionally well. Their center became known world wide and charitable trusts to help their cause were established in England, America, Spain, and even as far as China and Japan. Consultants of various specialties in medicine, Obstetrics and Gynecology, Pediatrics, and surgery came from these and far away countries to provide free medical service to the villagers and likewise donated money towards operations of the medical center.

In addition Kunsa Mori became an overnight author of endless string of books covering many areas of day-to-day life of the villager, medicine and romantic novels. Musu Jenela and Alexandro were endowed with three daughters, Famat, Bint, and Yat.

Famat, the elder became a doctor following footsteps of her uncle. While other two girls, Bint opted for law and Yat became comfortable with a nursing career. Alexandro said of Musu Jenela thus that if he had no eyes, his ears would love her invisible beauty; that if he had no ears, her outward features would move him.

If neither existed; he felt that just touching her would spark love senses in him. Simply he was blindly in love with this dame and because of true love he was able to forgive all her earthly faults. I hope this mirrors our own Alice in love land experiences or story.

Chapter 6

LOVE IN WARDS FIFTEEN

Normally in hospital setting romance would be the least one expect to rare its blindfolded head. This was what exactly transpired between Nurse Majula Seyabal and her patient Mr. Yaya Dibba. Shrieking Ambulance at top speed brought the Love Bird to the Manding Medical Centre, General Hospital's Accident and Emergency unit late at night. He had just suffered multiple injuries sustained from a headlong collusion with another vehicle coming from the opposite direction. Upon being resuscitated, fractures treated and stabilized Mr. Yaya Dibba was transferred to the Surgical Intensive Care Unit under the care of Nurse Majula Seyabal. Nurse Majula's fiancée had just left her, to paraphrase literally dumped her for a much younger and prettier lady not overly occupied by the call of her profession.

The situation left Nurse Majula Seyabal vulnerable and lonely. Many at first thought she was not ever going to be involved with men after her dumping into an old well the engagement ring her last fiancé had placed in her finger three months ago. Love is indeed blind as this story unveils.

Dr. Alhasan Sisawo Ceesay, MD

Brace up dear reader for love is true and true blind. Mr. Yaya Dibba woke up the next day and despite his trauma he was almost trying hard to regain his independence. Many times Nurse Majula and another juniors would assist in his bath, dressing, toileting and feeding. Dibba was a highly talented executive manager of his cosmetic company. It was the favorite shopping center for beauticians and upper class section of Njawara City in the Badibous, the Gambia. Thirty-year-old Nurse Majula Seyabal was a unique Nightingale in her own rights. She will go to extreme lengths to be at service to help fellow humans and loved every bit of nursing and dealing with the sick. At first she was almost an innocent bystander in the evolution of her relationship with Mr. Dibba. The phenomenon of love or true chemistry of heart at times evolves gradually. Mr. Dibba would not accept any other nurse wheel him into the garden or outdoors other than Nurse Majula Seyabal. Her colleagues observed the body language coming from Mr. Dibba but not her. She was just doing what her calling asked of her. Helping the sick and giving them as much comfort as can be possibly rendered without going beyond the bounds of duty or hospital regulation regarding patient, doctor and nurse moral expectations. Simply, unlike the Hollywood dramas, no flirting with patients or doctors was allowed behavior in the hospital environment.

It all started when one day Nurse Majula wheeled Dibba to his room. He asked to be left sitting in the chair but this was not appropriate for he might fall or develop pressure sores if left there too long. Dibba insisted that he could manage and besides the hospital staff is quite kind. He urged her go home and rest for the staff will help if he needed helping. However, Nurse insisted that she could at least help him undress and change to cleaner ones. He still insisted that he could manage. Nurse left his room reluctantly fearing to leave him in his helpless state. She blushed shamelessly, tears pricking her eyes as she made her way to the door. The tears and reason for it certainly surprised her. She heard the wheelchair move across causing her heart to almost bust through her chest for fear that he tumbled. "Nurse dear", he called. She walked towards him and he took her hand, looking up at her. He asked her to forgive him as he was wrong and worn out. He said, "You must be tired too. You have hardly rested since my admission and now here we are alone."He gave her hand a squeeze, and she had a sudden realization as she gazed down into his eyes, that, had he been standing he would have pulled her to him and kissed her. As it was, she could hardly bend down and kiss him for hospital rule forbade nurses falling romantically with their patients, although how she longed to kiss him.

As if he had read in her thoughts the echo of his own, he lamented and released her hand. Majula finally went home but became hounded by the spark that reared between her and Dibba. At first she tried to warn herself not to be overcharged by emotion or attachment she now developed for patient Yaya Dibba recovering fully from multiple fractures three months ago. She became possessed and obsessed by the compelling love that is growing between her and Dibba. She could not believe that she was falling in love after disappointment she just experienced from the hands of her former fiancée. Tormented by this restlessness she consulted a trusted lady friend Mami Suware about this development and asked if she should give it chance to fruition. Mami, advised her saying, "please follow your gut feelings about him and note your advancing age which, traditionally dictate that you be married at current age." It is now almost two years since Dibba had his accident and was discharged to the efficient care of the Physiotherapy Department at Orthopedics. Being in good hands accelerated his recovery. It went so well for him that he literally walks on his own with hands free of any walking aid. He no longer experiences stiffness or painful joints. Luckily, he sustained no spinal cord injury during the accident.

One would hardly recognize him for his features had return to normal because of his current miraculous recovery from an injury that would have lamed most. He kept interest in his future with the lady of his dream, Nurse Majula Seyabal. Dibba initially, before leaving college, cultivated contacts with influential families and with Baurocrats and officials at Njawara. Hence, it had not been a surprise when he succeeded in getting a permit to set up a government-subsidized shop, he styled, "FIRST AND LAST STOP GENERAL STORE & COSMETTIC" for retailing cosmetics and other commodities at controlled prices. This was Dibba's passport to prosperity and the business tycoon in the region. His was the only shop of its kind in the area. In addition to all sorts of cosmetics he sold rice, oil, tea, sugar, kitchen utensils and kerosene. People liked his business and patronized it well. He had no shortage of customers who believed that it was useless barging with Dibba for in the end he would with a tantalizing smile get exactly what he wanted. His thriving business, because of business acumens, eclipsed all others. One day lying comfortably on his divan a familiar figure crept pass by him. He at first thought that he might be dreaming for not far away and right before him was standing the lady of his dream worth any thing in life for him.

Initially he disregarded it and continued watching pigeons feeding by through his pair of silver-tipped sunglasses. Moments later, just when he was about to doze he heard a familiar voice. It certainly was that of Nurse Majula Seyabalo being cautious not to disturb his rest. She looked as in her first bloom of adolescence with a gentle, innocent, pretty, self-possessed in long African print dress. He was petrified by her beauty and cowed by tradition of shame and modesty that he barely glanced for fear of offending her. She at first wondered why he was holding back but then it occurred to her that they did not meet for almost a year since his discharge and that she kept limited telephone calls until she was sure that Dibba was her man and that things would not end up as her last fiancé did. There is a saying in Africa, which goes like this; "Old firewood no had for ketch", and it applies in this relationship. Soon Dibba, got up towering over the five foot two inches Majula, and said, "Hello dear. I never expected to see you so soon". He bent down to her. His lips were very close to hers now. "Do not worry about it now. All you have to do is to say yes I will marry you and you have Mr. Dibba as your slave for life". His lips touched hers and they kissed endlessly in joyful tears. Dibba said, "I could not ask you before while in hospital but now am much myself. What is your answer to my quest?"

A proposal of marriage from the incredible handsome and wealthy business tycoon was reason enough to upset any woman especially one that was thrown in favor of a younger prettier girl. Majula could not believe her stars and meaning of it for both. Should she accept the path of love or follow that of duty? She had made up her mind to become personally involved with her patient to the anguish of the Matron of the hospital. Majula realized that her true happiness lies with Dibba, a former patient of hers and reagent businessman. Majula's hand tightened on his. Words came from her lips, her throat being dried, faint words that can hardly be heard but Dibba understood and did not need to hear them. Their meaning shone in her star field eyes. He kissed her gently over and over and promised that they can plan their future as of the morrow. Majula returned hurriedly but very happy and reported to her confidant Mai Suware about what transpired on visiting her former patient. Everyone was elated by the news of Majula and Dibba getting married soon. She told her friends, "I have good reasons to marry him and the sooner the better for Dibba is filthy rich", drawing laughter and admiration from her friends. Both Dibba and Majula are very serine and quite natured people. Hence they selected a private wedding ceremony despite protest from friends on both sides of the isles.

They married quietly on the following Friday in simple ceremony and flew to London for honeymoon and a three months vacationing. Three months later Nurse returned with a belly full of baby twins for Dibba. It is said that "all is well that ends well", hence everyone at Njawara wished them a happy marriage life with good health and plenty more twins.

Dudu Ceesay, brother in green with family

Njawara Banti Yassin

GRANDMA AMINATA KASSA COUNSELS

YOUNG LADIES ON LOVE

Grandma Aminata Kassa was, unlike grandpa Bajoja, a shy charming lady that upholds culture and tradition to the hilt. She normally fills in these biweekly village meetings when grandpa travels. Today, under the spreading Mango tree, she tries her hand in rendering a very difficult topic to teenage girls.

The topic is about love and what it entails. No wonder girls from as far as fifty miles walked to attend this august gathering to hear the matriarch lady speak from the heart and from experience. She began the epic debate by assuring women that God loved them more than any for only through them and by them did He choose to perpetuate his creation.

This brought a broad smile and nodding in approval by all in attendance. One of the teenagers shouted, "tell them mum. Men think they are kings and women are treated as weaklings needing to crawl under their colossal feet and beg for crumbs". This also drew very loud supportive cheers from eager twenty first century teens who no long care much about the status co the old ladies where groomed.

Grandma with a half smile but stern faced calmed the crowd down and retorted that a world without a system is a void and that when women who are God's custodians of life play into the hands of the devil and bad playboys they ruin not only their lives but also the lives of generations to come.

She told the silent crowd, "love is very unique gift but full of emotion and tempestuous moments and one has to weigh and bravely wade through quite few phases of it". She said, "Real love is far from that of teenage infatuation with looks, wealth or strength. These attributes are far less important but today' get rich quick and famous has engraved the superficial aspects of life in teenagers to the detriment of marriage life and commitment to one's partner". She said "love is endearing and poets of all generations since Adam and Eve have written about it without being able to convey its full impact on the being.

Lovers love, mother's love, husband or father's love all spells a unique chemistry between individuals needing sincere, true and mature responsibility beyond anything they have yet been confronted in their short lives."She emphasized her point in saying, "Love is joy, is pain and most rewarding no matter how short it may have occurred for the partners.

Love is ecstatic and turns us into wingless angels. It is only love that makes women dare get pregnant and endure a nine months gestation of excruciating life, the last two hours of labor being having one foot in the grave while the other in tug of war to preserve life and the new arrival. Yes, for loves shake women give up their homes and move in with some stranger to start the circle of life all over again, and again.

Love can at times be a despicable enemy if the one women set their hearts on is not receptive or honest, caring, disciplined and true to them. Love is a deep ocean full of turbulent waves only perseverance and experience keeps one afloat. Women are renowned managers of love."She warned that, "Today's men have turned out devils for they have no compunction to use young ladies for whatever gains they could drive from your lovely features, popularity, athletic, and voice.

Do not let them set the agenda of your lives. Be strong, get educated and well prepared for the real world out there than rush into the lime light of flash photography and anorexic celebrity that does not last. Remember, easy come easy go. Hence these bad fellows pushing you into unholy ways will thrash you as soon as another more beautiful madden surfaces and in so doing have carelessly ruined your life for good.

Refuse to be caught in their enticing nets of glitters without worthy ends for you or your progeny. There has never been a Mr. Right nor will you ever find one. However, there is out there some decent bloke who would be willing to share most of your values and ideals in life and be ready to support you and the children that may surface. Let no one deceive you. Love is a two way emotional human phenomenons or contract and one must give all they are able and be tolerant as well as contributive to make it a fruitful union of hearts. Love fanes half and half attitudes because it outcome, the children, need love and unified committed parenthood to nurture the next generation."

At this juncture of the discussion an old man shouted in sarcastic tone and asked, "Is it not true that without men women would be left lonely beauties?" This caused more commotion in the crowd and letting many more men ventilate. The sage smiled and told the old man, "I remembered fully how you used to beg your wife's friends to convince her of you love. Hence the feeling is same for the genders only that women seem to be more forthright in exhibiting emotion than men. Solitude is enemy of the heart and no one desires it. We love and wished to be loved as long as we live."

She told the girls to refuse to be human flags that bad men take advantage because of greed, weakness and the disease of the Joneses. She said, "I urged you be happy with how God created you and seek what good you could or can get out of life for yourselves and community. You will never look like Jane or Gloria no matter how hard you may try for you also is an exceptionally unique beauty in this world."

Grandma warned that women must never be androids nor allow themselves be victim of unscrupulous men and industry. "The first real love is the self. One must not be too selfish to forget living and letting others live". She reiterated that, "life was as short and temporal as yesterday and one most live it in worthy fashion. She added that the young ladies have to come to conscientious, explicit and judicious means in making decision with whom to share and spend the rest of their lives." She said ladies, "be warned that beauty like petals withers with time and that beauty of heart was the best asset to have in life."

The teenagers nodded and hugged each other in solidarity and approval of the statement by the sage. In addition she told them respect and being aware of the pains of others makes life easier to handle. Respecting oneself allows others to treat you in kind.

Dr. Alhasan Sisawo Ceesay, MD

Most antisocial lack respect to begin with for if they do they will not engage in the type of mayhem and community destruction they cause society. Hence the sage warned the ladies "be loafers in life and you must try to be good to yourselves, peers, loved ones and community." She said the new trend is not breastfeeding. All animals breast feed because it is the surest source of good nutrition for the babies and provides protection against illness. Breast-feeding also help prevent early pregnancy that would deter growth of the baby at hand. Although neither a doctor nor healer she told the girls that none of these professionals would deny what she just out lined about breastfeeding. "These are fundamental facts no one can or is able to dispute". Some freaky girls shouted, "I can bottle feed my babies and keep my beautiful features". To this the old lady replied by telling the gathering that "anything artificial is not half as good as natural and that in the long wrong it's the effect on the baby that matters and not how women looked. Secondly, no one remains stagnant and change is a must and one must treat ones baby fairly and not fall for today's industrial falsehood." She added, "Walking naked in the street is not womanhood and that a good woman loves to preserve her dignity and so dresses with moderation."

She emphasized that the example women set is what their progeny picks up as normal or good behavior. To the future would be mothers she told another harbinger of love is motherhood. "This is intrinsic and intertwined with love. Motherhood is love in the highest order. Women are the only gender of the human species endowed with unique gift of bearing children. A bay in a relationship is the most gratifying reward nature gave women. With motherhood came the most challenging of challenges a woman faces in her life.

First, they embark on the trail of at times heartache and joy of finding a compatible loved one. There after comes the real challenge. No, not maintaining the relationship in the marriage but caring for that forming baby in the womb for as long as it takes for it to want to join the rest of mankind in the real world. Yes, the hormonal and figure changes and cravings that follow despite uncomfortable nausea and vomiting some experience, is a unique experience every pregnant women is fully conversant with.

Motherhood is not daunting but requires every aspect of our skills to ensure the survival of the new member of the house.In the interim during gestation Mr. Right or husbands goes into pretext that they too were undergoing some form of gestation.

Off course you will come to know better and would be fully aware of this falsehood. Only women of the human spiecy experience gestational changes and its outcome. The day of reckoning starts with labor, which is the most risky moment of pregnancy. When the liquid or show starts dripping and runs along their thighs accompanied with abdominal pain and painful contractions which create such high pressure in the head letting us believe it was going to split us into two halves.

In the last two hours of the labor phase of becoming a mother and after having maximum dilation, we now have one foot in hell earth and the other just hovering or trying to drop in the grave. The insurrection or distance between living and departing this life could be paper-thin. Yes, delivering a baby is a serious encounter and a few never made it or remained intact. Some need episiotomies to allow that humongous-headed baby to sail through.

The first cry of the newly delivered baby is the most melodious and exhilarating pleasure a mother's ear hears. The suckling and bonding is another unique experience babies give to their fledgling mothers." Grandma warned that motherhood was not all hunky-dory plain sail pleasures.

There was the challenge of dealing with the various stages of development of the child and the guiding of it away from danger. "Yes, nurturing is a challenge and if men were to experience labor they will never have sex or allow themselves to be pregnant again and again like women kindly do every two years.

The sleepless nights and diarrhoeas, ill health and toddler curiosity all make mothering a full time demand needing female expertise. The first three years and teenage years are most difficult to adjust to. In the former the child is fragile and needs us for every aspect of its life, as it remains helpless. Our love and care is prerequisite to its survival.

While in the later, the teenage years, the young adolescent, call it pseudo-adult, perceives he or herself as already matured even though you know better not to continue giving guidance. They seem to be more of experimenters with life and so need our patients and abundant love and guidance as they ply through to find their niche in this rough world. We should avoid double standards such as extolling them to do as we say but not do as we do, knowing that they will notice the cloak over our face and with it we lose respect and trust from them."

She admonished the girls to learn to leave better foot prints on the sand of time so that a fallen sister seeing could take heart. Hence they should set better examples to be harbinger of the future for their progenies. She told them to seek for wisdom and understanding. If they exalt their loved ones they will be worshiped by their partners in this life.

She summarized by letting the girls know that motherhood was the most pleasant gift to women as it was the only route to the perpetuation of the human specie. Women and only women had the gift and responsibility of continuing the human race. She admonished them to give their best to their children so that they remain perpetuated.

In addition the great sage Grandma Aminata Kassa told them that one had two choices in life. "One could be grateful for everything life gave or be resentful for everything done for them". She advised the future mothers to concentrate positively on what would be the most powerful thing they can do to attain or alter their lives in an appreciable direction.

She told them, "You are always valuable and worthwhile human beings not because someone said so or because you are successful but because you decided to believe it and for no other reason."

Njawara Banti Yassin

She emphasized that believing in oneself is love itself and soul of the individual. Grandma's evangelical, frankness, and sincerity were recognized hallmark admonishment coming from the village lady sage at Njawara flabbergasted the girls. "Awake! Awake to love;"Said the matriarch to her young lady audience.The night was setting in fast and because quite a few of the audience had long walks to distant villages to return she ended the discussion with a prayer for peace, progress and prosperity to all and promised to deal with, another form of love, parenting next time.

Dr. Alhasan Ceesay & Wife Fatou Koma-Ceesay

Chapter 7

SEYABALO JAITEH AND KENYIMA MANEH

Just the name said it all for Kenyima Maneh. He was a handsome fellow pursuing a medical degree at the University of Africa, Bansang, The Gambia. Seyabalo was a chemistry student with intention of becoming a pharmacist in Gambia upon completion of her studies. The two met at the behest of Lamin Koyo of Njakunda village also fellow student at the University of Africa. Lamin Koyo loved law and speaks about how he would one day become prime minister of the Gambia and would change all the laws to favor women.

This Seyabalo applauded and kissed him several times while at the same time throwing romantic glances at Kenyima. At first Kenyima did not take note of signals coming from her nor were her winks enticing. Seyabalo was beauty in her own right but not attractive enough to let Kenyima loose his heart or bearings and pay attention to her despite frantic efforts by her.

She was on the plump or heavy side but bent on taking her trophy. To which Kenyima eluded saying, "the bigger they are the easier they fall". This made the other ladies laugh heartily as they display anorexic if not cachetic figures.

Wrong as it would turn out ladies are very methodical and insistent when they are in love. One obvious way of getting Keyima's attention was by stepping in between him and other ladies in the room or simply flirtingly and interjecting into conversation she was sure the other lady would not like disturbed.

She got his mobile while Kenyima was giving it over the phone to another medical student. She even fanned a sudden abdominal pain to get attention from him or to put Kenyima's medical prowess to test. She refused for him to call the ambulance to take her to hospital. She instead opted going to the birth room from where she sent a polite text begging for Kenyima to drive her home for her to take local medicine sent to her by her aunt Nyimanding from Gambisara. You guessed it.

The doctor fell for the trap and decided to excuse himself in the service of patient Seyabalo Jaiteh. She surprised Kenyima on the way to her flat by behaving too lady like and intelligently which captivated Kenyima and set curiosity that would end up cementing them for two good years before things fell apart. However, let us look more deeply into the powers of women over men. Kenyima was not your street savvy fellow but was instead immersed in medical books and patient care.

He was once known as the no nonsense guy by his fellow medical students, especial the ladies with who he was in class. Some of that would change as all work and no play make Jack a dull guy according to Seyabalo Jaiteh. Upon arrival at her flat Kenyima helped her get to the room and immediately bid her goodbye. Even though it looked too brief a stay and to which briefness she paid little attention for wanting to convince the poor fellow of her sincerity in being sick.

On his way home she rang him and ask if Kenyima would be able to check on her the morrow. Kenyima accepted but insisted that it had to be after 6 pm. Seyabalo gladly conceded and daringly said "good night darling". Kenyima could not fathom where the familiarity surfaced to allow her address him in that manner. He thought he had been gentlemanly and not fresh at all.

He placed the mobile down and drove home. Again her last phrase, "good night darling", kept coming into his mind over and over into the wee hours of the night. It not only confused him but also bordered him because he was not going to have any hing disturb his studies or schedule. The next day he told his most trusted friend, Musolu Marie who told him that he is in love with the dame.

He denied it vehemently. Nonetheless he was well attired and on his way to be at Seyabalo's flat on the other side of town. 6.00 pm found him at her door with a handful of bouquets of lovely roses he bought for her on his way to fulfill a promise. Well, well, at the door was beautiful Seyabalo waiting eagerly for her knight in Armour to pick her to love lane. She opened the door and hugged him lovingly. It was such a hug he never experienced, plus a delicious kiss on the lips. This momentous act flabbergasted Kenyima.

No surprise that they were glued together by mouth by the time they reached the settee to repose. The kisses continued longer than expected. Then Seyabalo asked that they have dinner before heading to the cinema she was dying to see. She told her friends about her date unbeknown to Kenyima who had originally planned to stay for a brief time at her flat and head back to the library and continue reviewing Anatomy and his Harrison Text book of Medicine.

Well, womanpower over came him and they went to moves till midnight. Upon taking Seyabalo to her flat she pleaded that he spent the night. He did not fuss much and spent the night and was rewarded his first unholy honeymoon from a lady he would never thought such romantic whirlwind and tight bonds was possible.

He was treated to a king's breakfast and after a hot shower together he rang Musolu Marie and confessed that he was indeed in love with none other than Seyabalo Jaiteh. Meanwhile, the other rival ladies got envious of Seyabalo and tried to dissuade Kenyima to terminate the affair before it gets to a point of no return for both of them. According to them Seyabalo was "neither his class nor was her elephant size half presentable in public for the liking of his friends". Love being blind Kenyima rebuff them and backed his love for Seyabalo.

The affair peaked to a magical crescendo when the two lovebirds decided to room together in one of the bungalows owned by Seyabalo's uncle who was more than instrumental to have the relation move forward to fruition. Things went well but Kenyima would not propose marriage as Seyabalo pushes for it. He had planned to marry only when he becomes a consultant surgeon and on meeting the right lady. The speed at which Seyabalo got him to go through the current arrangement needed careful review before he committed himself to her. This became sticking point for behind the scene Seyabalo's family was urging her not to loose him to any woman at all costs. His profession would be an asset to the family and a pride for her.

Marriage became a sticking thorn or bee in the bonnet for these seemingly inseparable lovebirds. Like all good things they do not last long and are hard to come by. The relationship started to turn for the worst as Seyabalo tried to ward off any woman she thought was interested in her man. It got so bad that she accidentally picked a fight with Kenyima's sister believing that she was one of those trying to get women for her rightful man.

It was a great mistake on her side for blood is thicker than water. Kenyima warned her not to repeat or disgrace his family for any reason. He told her in no uncertain terms that there would not be anything between them should any of his family encounters the challenged she confronted his sister with out of sheer jealousy.

As legend has it Seyabalo miscalculated the sternness of the warning and had a row with none other than Kenyima's cousin. Seyabalo's fractious act made up Kenyima's mind and he summarily stopped seeing her and never allowed her to visit for any reason. No more fake illnesses or request for medical aid from her. It took Seyabalo ten months to almost a year before surfacing in public. She hibernated out of pure shame in realization of her inaccessible jalopy love and jealousy for Kenyima.

This was a man she was not ready to relinquish to any woman and in so doing lost him the best she had ever had in her life. In the end she lost fifty percent of her body weight and even the girls that tormented her felt sorry that they went as far as they did in splitting her relationship with Kenyima.

Dr. Alhasan S. Ceesay graduating from the American University of the Carribean School of Medicine 1992

Chapter 8

DAY OF THE MATCHMAKER

Matchmakers like people in search of a call are normally caught in a wild fire of passion to help free lonely hearts from the grip of fear and in so doing enables others to enter the magical romantic world. This type of help comes in as a call to matchmakers.

Most matchmakers are in one-way or the other are themselves lonely but rather push others into relationship than daring the social waves of maturity. They are desperately in love but could not make the first move to fulfill their impulses. Some matchmakers do it for monetary gains. Hence they go head over heels to get others hooked.

The matchmaker is extremely gratified when he or she succeeds in bringing love to others.Hence let us observe matchmaker Malang Bulafema and how he brought the coupling of Fafanding Fatajo and Miss Umie Pullo of sare Jarga village, Lower Badibou, the Gambia, West Africa. Events had it that Malang Bulafema and Fafanding Fatajo met after a day's work in the fields and where on the way home when they accidentally ran across Miss Umie Pullo. Umie is a beautiful twenty-three year old longhaired Fulani girl.

Malang instantly noted Fafangding's conversation stuttering and his gazed fixated on the girl. Sensing something very deep about the look Malang tested the waters by asking Fafanding if she was gorgeous and how he felt about her. He pushed his luck by asking if Fafanding would like her to be his wife.

Both questions took Fafanding by surprise knowing that Malang Bulafema was known in the village as master news monger and who most keep their secretes away from him to avoid being the talk of the day at the village Bantaba. Because of this laxity in Malang he was able to gain access into private yearnings of many villagers especially young women whose confidence he had more than most in the region. Elders fear him with their daughters, as he was perceived as the right hand of modern day Satan. Matchmakers were in those days perceived as people working for none other than the Devil and Satan.

Malang was instantly challenged by Fafanding's refusal to answer any of the above-posed questions to him. He knew that Fafanding's fancy has been tickled and he must continue searching for the threshold of Fafanding's pulses and his feelings about Umie Pullo. Umie Pullo is one of the darlings of Sare Jarga village.

She is courteous, very self-respecting, hardworking, and gorgeous young lady that any normal male would like her as a wife. No wonder her parents and elders of the village were mighty proud of her and the way she carried herself. Neither Fafading nor Umie ever had lovers but had many peer friends full of admiration for them. So would bringing this two untouched be a challenge or not? Malang had his foolproof plans on how to do exactly that. Having had his inclination as to how Fafanding felt by his refusal to answer question about Umie he turned on to finding Umie's views on men and who would be suitable for her as an ideal life partner. First he surreptitiously interviewed several known friends of Umie and learnt that beside respect for men Umie hardly had expressed anything of concrete desire about being enamored or even having a secrete lover at heart. She was according to her friends an angel in human flesh which opinion made lots of her peers sort advice from her and respected her views. She was through and through an honest young lady who hated lairs and loved her community.Malang had his work cut out for him for these two were the most challenging for him to turn into lovebirds. One thing he was certain was that it would be easier to penetrate Fafanding than Umie's heart.

He next befriended Umie's elder sister to gain more insight into the family and parental control if there was any behind Umie's strict no nonsense life style. The family welcomed him guardedly amongst them but kept their lips tight to avoid being quoted at the Bantaba the next day, week or months later for Malang Bulafema had a knack of getting information he wanted while his victims are unaware of being too gregarious.

Alas! Malang had now collected all the data he wished at his fingertips and went to work for his goal. At first most thought that Umie might have fallen for Malang Bulafema to allow or explain the open-door policy the family recently accorded him. Only he knew that not to be the case while he continued to lead all astray or on wild goose chases. This suspicious closeness to Umie made one of her uncles to interrogate Malang Bulafema about his recent closeness to the Pullo family and what were his objectives.

Being under the spotlight he confesses to having no desire or stake on Umie or any of the Pullo female members of the family but had some great news they and him would smile for at the end of the day. Malang Bulafema told his interrogator that it was too soon to spill the beans out but needed a few more moves before he could open up the Pandora's box.

Her uncle welcomed the findings and was, like the rest, more delighted and curious about what good news this undeclared broadcaster had on their beautiful girl. Umie was called to a family secret meeting to let the cat out of the bag. Umie assured them that she had no hidden secrete and was not keeping any from them nor does she know what Malang Bulafema had in mind.

Her innocent candor made them even wonder more as to what good news Malang implied when he met with Umie's uncle. Malang of all people now knows he has to tread his path gingerly in bringing the good news he promised about Umie. Hence he went to work on Fafanding to enable him peak up courage and tell how he felt about Umie.

Lo and behold Fafanding Fatajo had no one in mind other than this lovely Fulani girl Umie. It took Malang quite a juggling act to get Fafanding confess his inner yearning for any girl more so to admit love for this self carrying lady of Sare Jarga.

It came to light that the inclination started as far back as when Umie and Fatajo were tending sheep in the grassland at which time they actually sized each other but never came to giving in for pride and fear of defiling the names of their respective families.

Umie had once made some sort of move in teasing him any time they chance to meet but it never went beyond that village style of romance. They never held hand, kissed or were ever alone together as such proximity at their age was taboo. Fafanding had opened up to a distant uncle who died before fulfilling his promise of having a family meeting about his yearnings. Hence Fafanding kept his feelings to himself until the day he was walking from the fields accompanied by Malang Bulafema.

He was going to spill the beans out but on realizing Malangs' reputation he backed off to safe guard Umie's feeling for not being told but to hear about her unfounded engagement from nowhere other than the Banataba mouth to mouth broadcasting system.

Malang Bulafema armed with this fantastic success now encircled Umie. One day after the weekly meeting at the Bantaba he cornered Umie and told her of his findings and that Fafanding Fatajo had vowed to marry none other than her. She at first pushed it all aside for fear that Malang was on his rumor gathering tactics. Three days later she asked one of her friends, Sara Bah, if she heard anything about Fafanding Fatajo and some girl being rumored in the village.

The friend replied in the negative and chuckled at the question with peering eyes at Umie. Both girls laughed and went their ways but her friend became suspicious that Umie herself might be girl she was implying.

The plot thickens as Sara Bah also had an eye on Fafanding Fatajo but his refusal to reciprocate to her flirting convinced her that Fafanding might be impotent to cause him run away from girls any time he was approached. Umie asking her about Fafanding made Sara Bah double her attempts to draw Fafanding Fatajos' attention to her before she loses him to other girls in the village specifically Umie.

Malang on knowing this brewing battle of the brood decided to bring to Umie's attention the likelihood that her very best and trusted friend Sara Bah was about to steal the jewel of her heart right in front of her very eyes in bright day break. This infuriated Umie, as love being blind and jealousy it mortal foe. The two girls had an honest confrontation about poor Fafanding Fatajo who remained unaware of battle being waged in his name. This was the key moment Malang Bulafema prayed for as it added his leverage over both Umie Pullo and Fafanding Fatajo.

Now that he knew Umie's willingness to not to give Fafandin away Malang arrange a secret meeting without letting Umie or Fafanding knowing that the two will now be offered a face to face chance of speaking out their mind about the other or loosed forever from forest pray lurking in the woods.

Maland made sure he and Fafanding were at the meeting venue earlier than time he gave to Umie Pullo. She arrived head covered for fear of being seen with Malang in the bush. She was surprised at seeing Fafanding and almost dashed away out of shyness. It was Fafanding who politely begged her to stay for them to hear what Maland had to say and why he brought them together in this unusual manner.

She agreed after gathering her nerves and said, "go on tell us why this meeting and of all places it could take place". She loved Fafanding and was not about to miss the chance to talk things with him in this and time.

She is acutely aware of competition brewing up between her and Sara Bah, which she was determined to stamp out and cut it at the bud before an irreversible mistake occours. Malang asked Fafanding to open up and be a man by repeating what he told him about this Umie girl before the two of them and God.

Fafanding Fatajo with eyes on the ground, barely able to look into Umie's face directly, at first stuttered and then said, " yes, Umie its true I love you with all my heart and would feel blessed if you acquiesces to that wish of you becoming my wife following traditional norms."

Umie was filled with joy and tears of delight ran down her cheeks. She ran to hug him and said, "I too feel blessed having you my husband and future father of our children". It is said that a way to man's heart is through his stomach but a bouquet of red roses with a diamond engagement ring inserted in it is a sure way to catch a girl.

Well, Malang Bulafema has capped one more romantic success in his commitment of bringing love to seesawing hearts. The meeting resulted for the first time the pair walked holding hands until at the fringes of the village before Fafanding Fatajo told her that his uncle Sheriff Balajo and friends would soon start the ball rolling for their final union as man and wife.

On reaching home umie could hardly wait to tell her mother Hulay Ndong but begged her to keep it as strict secrete until the arrival and meeting of the Pullo family by Sherif Balajo and company.

Umie and her mother were delighted in silence knowing what was about to unfold for Umie and the Pullo family. A week went by before the expected delegates showed up at the door of the Pullo family. Samba Pullo, Umie's father, welcomed the guest and after normal formalities and lots of enquiries about each other's family's' health, Bachi Pullo, umies' uncle asked the guest what was their mission to cause them call upon the family on that glorious day of the year of love.

Sheriff Balajo wasted no time in letting the Pullo family know that they have been asked by their son and nephew Fafanding Fatajo to come and asked for privilege of having the hand of their daughter Umie Pullo in marriage to Fafanding Fatajo. In response Bachi Pullo said, "Let us first take a glass of palm wine as it makes men eloquent and give love to tame women."

All laughed after the libation. Bachi Pullo told the delegate that the Pullo family would discuss the good news and wish of their nephew Fafanding Fatajo after consulting Umie Pullo about it. A reply will be sent through the family scribe in two days. They again greeted, shook hands and Fafanding's envoy departed hopeful and happy they were given listening ears indicating that Umie had not been engaged or chosen to marry a family friend.

At dinner, Bachi Pullo convened meeting of the elders of the family with Umie, her mother Hulay Ndong, aunts along with elderly ladies who had historical ties with life of the Pullo fraternity. They were all extremely delighted and honoured hearing the request from Fafanding Fatajo but all agreed that only Umie could, and rightly so, could give the response everyone assembled awaits.

Aunty Awa Pulbe got up, spat the tobacco she filled her mouth up and said "It was her aunty duties to ask the young lady before them if she loves the fellow requesting her hand in marriage knowing that he was no Fulani but a good mandinka." Inter tribal marriages are rare especially between Fulas and the Mandinka. Hence she must here and now tell them how she feels about this and if need be request time to think but they must know before two days as promised to Sheriff Balajo.

Umie got up and bravely addressed her father, mum, aunts and elderly friend of the clan. She told them, "I was more delighted than any of you for this was light at the end of tunnel and have been praying for God to grant the wish that she would meet a man she loves and loves her in return. Fafanding Fatajo's heart and hers' were intertwined into one soul.

She loves him dearly would marry him right away if the family bless her wish and request". She requested their indulgence and sat down and waited for formal approval from her family. The clan was happy to hear her wish and have blessed it unreservedly because Fafanding Fatajo was well liked in the village and his family not only being historical friends of the Pullos but had always come to their aid if needed and attend and participated in any event involving the Pullo family.

Hence, without any objections being raised by all present Bachi Pullo, told her "We conquer with you and pray that this union of hearts and friendship yield even more fruitful rearwards for the two families.

Samba Gaulo, the Pullo family scribe, was then asked to report the outcome to Sheriff Balajo and the Fatajo family so that discussions could start on the dowry and setting of the wedding date.

Early in the morning of the next day Samba Gaulo and an assistant priest went to tell Sheriff Balajo of the good news that the Pullo family gladly acquiescent to his nephew Fafanding Fatojo marrying Umie Pullo and that his side should now arrange for time of discussions pertaining to the dowry and setting of the wedding date.

Njawara Sheriff told Samba Gaulo, "Kindly convey our joy in hearing their response to our hearts' desire and to tell the Pullo family that the Fatajos were more than delighted for this continuing gesture of friendship and trust and that discussions would start sooner than expected after he conveys this fantastic news to all concerned.

Africa being steep in tradition allows cordial ironing out of important matters in the family, among friends and even with adversaries. The family met and agreed on a set dowry to discuss knowing the Pullo family like cattle more than diamonds.

Friday a week after consultations the two families met at the home of a respected village elder to debate, iron out differences and arrive at mutually acceptable dowry to enable marriage of Umie Pullo and Fafanding Fatajo. It was at the end agreed that the Fatajo family pay a dowry of twenty cattle, twenty bushels of maze, ten goats, and loads of dresses and presents Umie would demand.

This was considered reasonable knowing the attachment of Fulani's to animals. The more cattle they boast about the more social standing they become. In short is power and this was the best time to get as much of it as can be before the nut is tied between Umie and Fafanding.

The Western minded would cry out foul in believing that the whole fiasco was a deal selling Umie and never catered her interest. In Africa parents love their children and do break their backs for them during their growing days. In addition marrying away does not end the relationship or the family's contribution to the welfare of the kids as happens in foreign cultures.

Hence the stronger their stand at old age the better they can continue to be of help. Dowries are considered as the child's part contribution to what the Western people recognizes or call pensions reward for the family. The cattle and goats can always be sold at hard times. Certain numbers of the animals are normally earmarked for the bride in the event she may need help due to poor yield or for treatment of some sort.

Barring the surfacing of any objection or any reasonable alibis for annulment and dowry being paid the date for the wedding is set. The village scribe, town crier according to Western cultures, is asked to announce the good news to all in the village, hamlets and others far and wide as possible to draw maximum participation in the ceremony. A Friday is selected and the elders, priest along with the two families, friends and celebrants all join in to anoint the marriage between Fafanding Fatajo and Umie Pullo before the eye of God and her parents.

Now both peers of the couple pitch in to help the preparation for the forthcoming wedding ceremony. The fellow's family, brothers, sisters, aunts and uncles, and companions all pitch in to make it a memorable wedding festivities and night to remember.

Upon the completion of the mosque activities the bride and groom are allowed visitation and his friends usually accompany the groom. On the day of the real marriage ceremony the whole village and nearly all the neighbouring villages gather to participate in the event. Umie in her tribe's bridal dress and costume becomes envy of her lady peers.

There is drumming and dancing all day until late in the evening before the bride enters the grooms house accompanied by elderly village women. The husband or his friends help her cross the so-called threshold. The friends leave them alone for the night. The ecstasy this night of the honeymoon and day could never be matched by any other occasion other than the birth of a child. The couple can now stay permanently together, for better or worst as husband and wife.

The ceremony usually continues up to dawn before the younger celebrants retire. The bride keeps on her bridal attire for at least two weeks before shedding them for good.

Most women store these special dresses for life, giving them only to their daughters if they cannot get their own. The saying that, my wife is mine and I do with her what I want dose not exist in a village setting. Here family and community are the basic fiber of life.

Hence, there are a host of irreconcilable differences between traditional Mandinka cultures and their western counterparts. Malang Bulafema let a shy of relief having bagged this union of hearts in his archives and was triumphant in telling Bachi Pullo that what he just witnesses about Umie was due to his relentless effort and believes that these two lovebirds were tailor made for each other.

He wished them a happy marriage life and the best of health in days, weeks and years to come. Bachi Pullo stood in amazement abound with the highest regards for persistence and sense of worthy purpose as exhibited by Malang Bulafema in the above saga. It made him now disagree with all the rumors about this matchmaker and let the scene happy that it all end well for both sides and people were dead wrong about Malang the matchmaker of the day at Sare Jarga.

Chapter 9

MY SPANISH HULA MOCHA CHA-CHA!

Alex was at work early morning when some premonition of good feeling greeted him. From the blue came the most beautiful Spanish lady who entered his shop catching his eyes if not his fancy. Alex at first tried to brush his feelings aside and just took her as one of many pretty faces that normally walk the isles of the shop.

Why then did this stuck in his mind's eyes? Why now and not when he asked Jane out but was unfairly and thoughtlessly turned down instantly? The smiles, courtesy and unique beauty and body form made this one stand out above all that ever stepped into this shop.

His heart beat faster and faster as this mirage of beauty approached to ask for price of scarf she picked out. He could not believe his unfolding luck as the beautiful Spanish madam approached him. "Hello dear. How much for this scarf and dress?"

The sound of a soft melodious and romantic voice swept Alex off guard and made him remained stunned for a minute or two before he could stop looking directly into her lovely face and told her "for you twenty pounds would do."

She said, "O ma mea this is good price", and paid for the dress and scarf. She introduced herself, "I am Miss Trejo Sanchez from Spain. What is your lovely British name?" Again, Alex could not offer an answer immediately for being petrified by her beauty and by her seeming to be interested in him.

He pinched himself and summoned courage and nervously said, "I am Alex Good but friends just call me Alex. Hence you too can call me Alex". The mirage jokingly asked, "Are you then Alexandra the great of England I kept hearing about?"

Both laughed over the joke and Alex for the first time in dealing with ladies offered his contact card, requested her look at his website and asked her to visit again sooner than later. She smiled and on leaving gave a last romantic glance at Alex before disappearing into the street.

Alex ran to the door just to have another look and vous la she was at the bus stop and she turned to look and waved at Alex before boarding. She shouted out at the bus wind, "I will surely come again. Perhaps we will see Saturday next." This left Alex flabbergasted and more than delighted. He work effortlessly through the day intermingled with love songs through the long day.

It was Thursday and for him Saturday seemed years away as he started contemplating on how to approach her. Would trying a little Spanish lingo, as king Henry's poor French did for Katrine at the battlefield in Arginecort help forge a relationship for them? What sort of dress should he wear or would it be okay to ask for a date in these early days of their meeting? These and many more questions filled his mind to the point that coworkers noticed the joy emanating from him and started to tease Alex about meeting a new bird they all wanted to know but he would not reveal the secrete. Came Saturday, Alex was the first to report to work and in three piece suit with marching shiny shoes that mirrored his heart.

The staff reminded him that it was not his birthday yet and asked if he was going to a wedding or a blind date with madam miracle. Laughter pervaded for a while before everyone settled to his or her post for the day. Alex mean while kept on humming love songs from ancient to current top songs. Soon at noon walked in beautiful Spaniard looking stunning lady in her Spanish dress. She greeted and handed a perfumed red rose to Alex while keeping one to her. The staff applauded several times in approval and now saw why Alex was in such attire before the start of the weekend. Alex thanked and kissed her on the cheek with courtesy for wanting to maintain his mature maleness and respect from his staff. Alex was manager of the shop and had cautioned against flirting with customers while at work. Now the hen has come to roost at his back yard. To avoid breaking his own rules he asked the staff to allow him a thirty minutes break to speak to his visitor at the staff lounge. They did because they never saw Alex with women and to see him that happy and committed was history in the making.

The two, Alex and Miss Trejo Sanchez walked through a throng of singing jubilated staff to mark approval and well wishes for them. Alex was touched to the core for solidarity he never thought he had from the staff. As for Miss Trejo Sanchez she just smiled through and entered the lounge room with Alex.

The two walked into the lounge and sat near each other on the sofa. A little silence followed before Alex broke the ice and offered cold soft drinks, as alcohol was not allowed during working hours, He told her, "I have never met a more prettier or beautiful lady than you and that he was flabbergasted by you stunning looks and admirable character. Miss Trejo Sanchez smiled in appreciation of the comments and said, "You too looked great and broad chest and strong looks and met the liking of women." It was then that Alex asked how long she was to stay in Britain and would she keep in touch. She replied, "I am leaving following Monday." And as such they decided to meet Sunday at Restaurant d'Amour to finalize their wish before her departure to Spain.

They held hands and kissed little bit and had to get to the shop as more costumers queued in needing Alex who had the keys to the till in his pocket. The beauty from Spain stunned even the customers. She waved goodbye to Alex and walked happily to board the bus calling Alex on the way to her hotel. Sunday, Alex bought a bouquet of roses with a gold ring and some cash in an envelope for her to take with her on the trip back to Spain.

Ladies seem to cry when surprised by good acts of love from men. And sure enough when Trejo Sanchez took her seat at the table and Alex had the waiter hand over the flowers to her and which said "From Alex madam!" She kissed him and broke down to tears of joy as she glanced the content of the envelope. Alex retorted by letting her know this was to reinforce what they had discussed at the shop and that she has as much time to think about it as pleased her before giving him an answer. Trejo Sanchez would have said yes to his request there and then but just nodded knowing Alex being a principled man would not push a decision on anyone and who then later regrets doing so.

They chatted and laughed over a lovely memorable dinner. It was the start of many such contacts for these lovebirds. Alex drove her back to her hotel and then returned happy to his flat sixteen miles away. Monday, Alex took time from work and took her to the airport. Miss Trejo Sanchez felt herself a lucky woman to have met Alex. She would do all she can to keep and perhaps marry him if he loves her enough to let her bear his children. Alex was back at work and three hours later a call from Spain came through the office line as he had asked.

He shut the door of the office and said "darling I am missing you already. How was your flight? Are you home now? Give my regards to your family and tell them I am looking forward to meeting them soon." This last bit elated Trejo Sanchez for it grantees that their meeting was not to be a one night stand affair and that there is promise in him wanting to meet her family. She said, "Darling I am forever yours. You are already etched in my heart.

I will convey your greetings and tell my family of your desire to meet them soon. Please darling, do it sooner than later". Both laughed as she confirms that it was to let him know she taught about him all through the flight from Manchester to Spain. She let a kiss and the phone went dead before Alex had time to return his.

He almost called back but had to hold back to avoid being pushy or acting infatuated. Back in Spain, Trejo Sanchez told her family and friends about her encounter with gentleman Alex Good and how lucky she must have been going to the shop at Wilmslow Road in Manchester, England. Unlike most ladies of her age who would have bought more costly fancy dresses with money Alex gave her, Trejo Sanchez decided to instead renovate her father's house to the surprise and delight of the family. This gave more liking to and approval for Alex's proposed visit to Spain. Miss Trejo Sanchez knows how to ply her way through the family's heart and in doing this she has gained their approval without them ever seeing or meeting Alex in the flesh.

Three month passed before Alex could pay a short three-day visit to his would now be his fiancée Miss Trejo Sanchez. The family and friends welcomed him into their midst with pride and gratitude for selecting their daughter.

Many Spanish dames thought Britain's Alexandra the great was worth competing for. Yes, they too would not let their paws off him and so was Sanchez who discovered him. Luckily Alex was not a ladies man and was contended with having Miss Trejo Sanchez than those currently throwing themselves a la cart to him.

A special welcoming party was done for him on the second night of his visit. At which he took the opportunity of proposing to Miss Trejo Sanchez. Off course it was for gone certainty between Sanchez and Alex but to stop the vying from going over board it was apt for them to declare their interests and intentions towards each other for all to know and wish them well.

He did this in grand style. When everyone was enjoying himself orshe or talking about how lucky Trejo Sanchez was in getting such a rich and handsome gentleman willing to marry a village local girl. It left the men envious of him and now trying to wrest from him what some thought belong to the Spanish community.

Well, as tradition will have, Miss Trejo Sanchez's uncle asked for the attention of all those present to hear pleasant news their chief guest has to tell them. Alex unabashed walked to the center of the massive ornately decorated hall and called Miss Trejo Sanchez to join him.

Then and therein he knelt and simply held hand and said "I would be the luckiest man on earth if you agree to be my humble wife." It was typically British style in brevity and to the point. Overly happy Trejo Sanchez looked straight into his eyes and she said, "For good or bad, in health, in sickness or in wealth you remained etched in my heart. It belongs to no one except us."

She then kissed him several times while Alex slipped an engagement into her finger. She lifted her hand high in the air, as if to tell the vying ladies and dames that she has warn at last. The crowd ruptured into frenzy applause and dancing continued to wee hours of the night. The next day their engagement became headline in most of the city's newspapers.

Trejo Sanchez was pleased and Alex became an instant celebrity he never envisaged while in Great Britain. He has become part of family and tradition different to his. He does have full support of his family, friends and coworker back home.

They spent the third day visiting historic areas and attended another party made in recognition of their joyful moment. They even went to watch the Matador fight very fires bulls before Alex boarded his flight to the United Kingdom latter that day. The life of celebrity is full of suppresses as Alex soon found out. At Manchester Airport where some Spanish journalist waiting to welcome him home and get some spook for their readers in England.

Alex was dumbfounded by this desire and being a private individual he wanted nothing like it. He now has to play cool to avoid being branded stiff upper lip aloof Brit by the newsreader eager to have a word or two with him about his bride to be in Spain.

He gave a short interview to all journalists of various papers but refused to reveal date of their marriage ceremony. He just let them know they would be among the first to know when the time comes. He thanked them. Leaving everyone pleased whiled he rushed home.

His own hometown had another surprise waiting for Alex. They let him return to spend the night quietly but by 7:00 Am a sweetheart message was left at his door with delivered flowers. The letter came from non-other than the city Council inviting him to attend a civic ceremony in his behalf on the weekend. Can Alex, the quite businessman absorb these entire celebrity thing and have normal life? He summoned his will and cooperated as fully as he can humanly tolerate without breaking down.

These were mere harbingers compared to what might take place on the days or weeks of his marriage ceremony. So far he is faring on well and had full understanding of his staff at work where some journalists decided to camp to have chance to talk the great Brits' Alex.

Friday that weekend, both the Chamber of Commerce and City council gathered to serenade Alex on his new world and soon to unite Britain and Spain. They would not like to be left behind or out done by any outside group. He was their full home grown Brit that deserved to be serenaded by council.

It took place as announced amidst lot of speeches and praises of the contribution this trades' man citizen was making to bring commercial as well as future tourist attraction to the city. Politicians seem to fall for media attention. The very advent of attention given to Alex, a simple businessman made city council and chamber of commerce of his town to cash in to catch some of the limelight.

They did not care if it was wise use of taxpayers' money as long as their faces appeared in headlines of the next day newspapers. Hence the serenading went on but it brought a big surprise as an after mirth effect.

Some of regretted having sailed along for three months later the aging 70-year-old mayor of the city resigned on grounds of poor health. Soon friends and supporters of Alex for mayor and the newspapers rushed to put Alex's name for the replacement of the retired mayor.

At the end of the by-election Alex had 76% of votes cast and became the 99th Mayor of the city. It sounded my like Alice in wonderland fairy tale but it really took place in the year of our Lord 1998.

Four months after Alex's mayoral inauguration he slipped quietly to Spain and had a private marriage ceremony at a secrete location with close family and friends attending.

The couple continued to have their honeymoon in New York unannounced. For the first time now Mrs. Trejo Good would have time to be with her husband without intrusion from newsmen and advertising companies wanting his photo or signature to attest to quality of product whose source was never too clear to him.

Alex too the above private ceremony because he had reached point of saturation with media intrusions and endless requests for interviews or photos cession to be used for commercial clips on products he had no idea of their origin.

All is well that ends well. This simple couple lived their lives as peacefully as could be had without changing attitude or becoming aloof due to post. They were blessed with two boys and three girls at the time I got interested in their story.

Chapter 10

LOVE LANE PARK

This lovers' paradise is located in Flint Michigan, United States of America. Our story goes as far back and starts in May 1964 when Martha Gardner met Willie Shepard and the two perambulated leisurely until reaching a bench at a quite corner of Love lane Park where their hearts would permanently be glued together. Hope the saga of this lovebirds will let us into secretes of Love lane Park. Willie Shepard was forty years old, was never married but maintained relationship with his high school girl friend until her passing twelve years ago. The departure left him in solitude and he directed his energies into producing the most successful international business firm, which he served as its founder and Chief Executive Officer. Martha Gardner was in her late thirties and an Assistant mathematics professor at the Community College in Flint. She had been married but had no children in that marriage.

She was widowed two years ago and had since never desired or been involved in romantic orientation until today when she laid eyes on Willie Shepard. Her feeling about him heightened and she started asking herself if this was the Mr. Right she longed to meet after her husbands' death? Would he love and care for her? Is he a playboy tycoon as business leads into most men? Willie being the older kept his cool and did not spill out his feelings, as he wanted to know more about this beautiful black queen.

As it is most black men are scared of developing relations with highly educated or call it qualified black ladies for fear that they will steal the limelight away from them and likewise become too bossy. Hence it was Martha Gardner who broke the ice by belling the cat with serious of questions regarding Willie Shepard and type of women, if any, he had been dating. He answered as much of the questions thrown at him as honestly as he could. Martha Gardner's quarries intrigued him and he suggested they think about the vibes emanating between them at that moment.

He told her, "I am having a rare but positive feeling for you and that I indeed liked you lot." while avoiding the use of the sacred word "love" on the first day of meeting a lady. Martha Gardner too sensed something magical and intriguing about him and liked what she heard and manner in which it was delivered. They walked around hand in hand for quite a while at the same time throwing wild romantic glances at each other. Soon the cell phone rang and, his secretary reminded Willie that he was to attend a church meeting in the next hour. It got Martha Gardner a bit concerned but Willie allayed her fears and said, "It was his secretary reminding him of commitment he made two weeks ago and had only taken few minutes break before attending when he ran into her. He needed her company and contacts where feasible." This he assured her was the best thing that had happened to him since the departure of his high school girl friend. He offered to drop her to the college before proceeding to the meeting Martha Gardner declined saying, "I would rather take little more time in the Park and fresh air while I ruminate over the good fortune of the day."

Willie concord and drove away to the church some twelve miles away. He thought of her all through the short trip. And guess what they called each other more than eight times before surrendering to romantic events of the day.

Martha Gardner took the bus home and on entering her room jotted the following in her diary "Met Mr. Right. Will keep him for I love him dearly." She continued to the shower and while there she still could no control her mind and image of Willie taking shower with her. She sang her heart deliriously for having met someone she likes and loves her.

While over a simple meal she got from the fridge her cell phone rang and sure enough it was Willie. His voice stumbled little bit but it came through and desired. He said, "Darling I just had to call for I could not stop thinking about you. My life would be blessed with you being in it. I already told my best friend, Dr. Garry Mathew, MD, about you and my feelings. He is very much encouraged about us."

Martha Gardner then read her jottings about the day to him and threw a romantic kiss over the phone. The two spoke their hearts as if children given ice cream the first time in their lives. They each promised not to loose the other and would do all they can to let this feeling mature to fruition to both. At the end of their three hours telephone talk Willie broke the news of him having to fly to Europe the next for business deals and meeting but would be back in two weeks time.

Martha Gardner half hazard wishes him bon voyage and that expects to see him in one piece sooner than later. Both laughed heartily and went to sleep. Early next day Martha wrote in her diary, "Can I accommodate such impromptu trip akin to business men? Would he fall in love with another lady just as he did with me? I will hang on and keep him persuaded that I am the best for him while others are mare impostors and opportunists." In class her students noticed lightness and joviality she never displayed before until her meeting Willie Shepard.

Good things are hard to come by and they too agreed that this businessman was her king of hearts in the making. In real and true love from the heart people do not instantly jump into bed. They first tied loose ends and when all was one; they can then have sumptuous honeymoon after wards.

Thise two weeks Willie Shepard being away will give both chance to reflect upon the vibes and sensual feelings they have toward each other. It will help clarify for both if this would be beyond a one-time affair coming from an accidental meeting at Love lane Park. So far Martha Gardner has doubts of her being able to adjust to a globetrotting lover. Only time and the two weeks absence of Willie Shepard would tell.

As for Willie he would have wedded her instantly but he is still keeping cool to learn more and to find out if she can assail her fears about his trade and travels. Both are exposed to people by virtue of their profession but Willie Shepard's is more tenuous for ladies to accept.

Nonetheless in one of Martha Gardner's reposed moments at Love lane Park a bigheaded mulatto with a brand new special made cardiac packed not far from the bench she sat. He walked to her and asked, "Can I have a word or two with you?" Her response was terse. She asked, "What is it you want to tell or seek from me?"

He came out directly and told her, "I am enamored and deeply in love with you." Martha did not know that Dr. Garry Mathew was Willie's friend testing her commitment to Willie Shepard. To make matters worst he threw a wad of hundred dollar bills at her lap and told her, "You can have it and use it unconditionally." This infuriated Martha Gardner and she came out fuming at him.

She told him, "You put his wad of money in x and y places of your own. Willie Shepard is my love and man for the rest of her life and no joker like you will make a fool of me to course me to loose a good thing I had. She told him, "You take your black x away or I will call the police to arrest you for being a nuisance and disturbing me."

She assured him saying I could go to the bank and have legitimate amounts ten times yours and retain my Willie Shepard." Please know that I will tell my man who definitely will put you in your correct mulatto place." Dr Garry Mathew was happy to find that Willie Shepard had found a lady who is committed to him and not the welcome mat of Love lane Park's one nightstand crowd.

Just when the doctor was about to leave Willie Shepard called from Germany and was told about the incident. His Doctor friend had told him in advance of the test he would put her through to test her loyalty and trust worthiness. Willie asked to speak with the perpetrator but he had already left as arranged.

He calmed her and promised to return shortly as some of the meetings have been cancelled. He would be at her side in two days time. Three days later Martha Gardner's Knight on a white horse arrived with lots of presents and a confession to make to her.

At her flat and on his knees he apologized for the incident by his most reliable friend Dr. Garry Mathew, the mulatto who accursed her the other evening at the Park. He told her, "It was purely my idea, for a true and reliable friend of his to check the suitability of the woman I intended to marry."

Knowledge that he loves her enough to want to marry her and the testing of her commitment to him made her happy and forgiving of the incident. She told him to remember what goes round comes back to hunt one. She too has very beautiful dame friends who might test the waters for her. He challenged her to try at the same time assured her that let her bring them on.

He said, "I have seen many more since the death of my girl friend but never fell victim of theirs' until when he met her." This really reassured and calmed her and they had a splendid evening together before Willie took off to his office to prepare report of his European trip.

A week later Doctor Garry Mathew and Willie Shepard visited her together because the doctor wanted to apologize and reaffirm his support for the love she has for Willie. Apology was duly accepted and the wad of money being represented to her by Willie Shepard. They even had joint photos taken before finishing the evening at a cinema with the great doctor's wife Mrs. Elaner Mathew tagging along.

The two ladies gelled and laughed over tricks men play on those ladies they care about. Mrs. Elaner Mathew told how her love used his sister to make her jealous about him.

It was only late in the relationship did she come to know that the sister was indeed his twin partner and they enjoyed playing rascal games on angels like her. Now that both parties are acquainted and comfortable with each other the ladies became sisters that shared secretes and jokes.

To Martha Gardner's delightful surprise Willie Shepard announced that henceforth he would delegate his assistant to be traveling to not so important conferences for he wanted to spend more time with his charming Martha Gardner.

Martha became a must guest in many and almost all business ceremonies. Willie Shepard's church appointed her head of the women group and organizer of church wedding activities. The relationship with Willie opened a Pandora's box that made her known and more popular icon than Willie Shepard who was always business like unlike light and easygoing Martha Gardner.

Today, she is a lady Deacon at the church for her input was well appreciated by the members.

Willie, as usual in dealing with matters concerning him, took his time before he proposed to Martha Gardner. He wanted to be certain the fame being her accolade would not get to her head and change her into a monster instead of the gentle, kind and loving lady he met at Love lane Park.

He requested her hand in marriage in his own style and time. Hence with few friends tagging along he walked with Martha Gardner up to the bench he found her on their first day of their meeting; sat her and then after few minutes took out the most beautiful diamond ring, knelt by her and said "Honey my love for you is infinitum and I will be the luckiest man on planet earth if you would marry me at your chosen time and space." Stunned Martha Gardner could only, with joyful tears welling and dripping all over her face, say, "I do love you and would be the happiest lady in town being your lawfully wedded wife." Friends took photos of them kissing and Willie Shepard promised to have the priest announce their engagement at the next Sunday service. It pleased Martha for her lady friends would not like to be left out in anything so pleasing about her and in her life. Love is said to be blind but in the case of Professor Martha Gardner and business tycoon Willie Shepard it was not blinded but wide-eyed in bright daylight. Love has etched or glued their hearts forever enchantingly together.

The students in her class along with staff at the Community College were even more delighted for her than she ever expected for her pupils to show solidarity with a teacher. It was about end of term. And guess what? The class decided to throw a party in her and Willie's honour. On the day of the party, the college band provided music renditions ranging from Motown, Diana Rose's "We will meet again" to Beethoven and Batch.The staff brought gifts and flowers to serenade the soon would be couple. It was a touching affair and one of the most pleasant hours ever at the college. Everyone enjoyed him or herself and was eager to know the actual day of their tying the knout. This they kept a guarded secrete and each gave a heart felt thanks to the staff and students for sharing the joy with them. Willie promised to inform the school as soon as all formal decisions are ironed out. Many a heart bled at love lane Park just as many more return there fifty years after they were proposed to by their Knight in love on a white horse sweeping their feet to chimes of wedding bells.

The years have witnessed a billion tear drops of joy welled at Love lane Park in Flint Michigan. For better or for worst it has turned out to be the match making zone of Flint.The deacon's engagement to Willie Shepard was welcomed at the church leading many ladies to envy her. Two months later they announced the date of their wedding ceremony to be held at the dancing Tabernacle. The venue was chosen for numbers expected attend would not fit in their small three hundred year old church of Christ. Hence the huge ornate church or Cathedral was apt for the occasion and grandeur to marking of Martha Gardner and Willie Shepard. By noon of the weeding day the above massive opulent cathedral's hall, seating more than 1000 was full to capacity. Marriage between two very popular icons drew almost a quarter of Flint into attendance of the ceremony. Those who could enter the cathedral lined the route just to have glance and to wave at the newly weeded and to remember their' some months ago or years gone by. Also classic cars in their hundreds drove through to deliver guests to the ceremony.

This scenery befits the English royal wedding and reminded the older spectators of HRH Princess Diana's wedding to HRH Princes Charles of England. The hymnals, singing, praises and clapping black style could be heard miles away and throngs in the swayed and or danced while singing their hearts out with pleasure.

When all in the Cathedral were seated, priest, well attired Willie and friend with the wedding ring besides him the piano plaid the wedding match or tune for Old-man Joe and Martha Gardner to be present and for to take her marriage vows in the presence of God and community. On arrival old man Joe kissed Martha Gardner and stepped aside for the ceremony to start. One could not fail to notice the joy and wide-brim smile on Martha's face on her final of spinsterhood and the taking of a new and would be most rewarding marriage for her and Willie. She had been here before but this one between her and Willie Shepard meant more as it found her a much matured woman, and having had time to compare the pros and cons.

Where as in the previous marriage, she jump into it girlish fashion without much reasoning through it and above all she did it at the time to purely please mum and dad who thought it was time for her to be wedded. This one is hers and Willie Shepard was love itched in her heart. Every thing about him gives her immense pleasure she could live with.

Alas! She was happy to take her vows and done Willie Shepard's wedding ring till death do they part. My dear reader now arrives the moment of truth when the priest offered prayers and then asked if there be any in the congregation who could give reason why the two before them should not be wedded couple. He urged him or her speak out or forever hold their peace to allow proceedings of the wedding.

None came forth and so Willie Shepard and Martha Gardner took their vows amidst broad smiles and endless kisses upon being told by the priest that they can kiss.The people applauded and sang praises to God and to the couple for this joyful and lovely day for the now newly wedded.

With the veil removed, Martha Gardner, now Mrs. Shepard, looked ravishingly beautiful and her wedding dress remains talk of the town for many, many moons. The motorcade to wedding reception hall was jammed with flowers and presents from on lookers. The flowered hall down town was spectacular and people thronged as before to see the couple. Flowers, rice and greeting cards were thrown at them as they slowly drove through throngs of well-wishers and friends in Flint, Michigan. Long speeches were made by numerous of the wedded and people shared delicious cake from the four feet tall wedding cake specially prepared by Flint's best wedding caterers. At the end the couple flew to Edinburgh in England to have their honeymoon in private at one of the many castles in that city. Very few weddings matched the popularity of this Love lane Park's couple. They returned three weeks later to their various occupation much happier and ready for the their jobs than ever before.

Two years on Dr. Gary and Mrs. Elena Mathew named their third child after Martha Gardner. This further cemented their friendship and twined the ladies.

The fairy tale of Love lane Park yielded many lovely children between Martha and Willie who are still married and in their sixties. They too reciprocated and named their only daughter after dear Mrs. Elena Mathew.

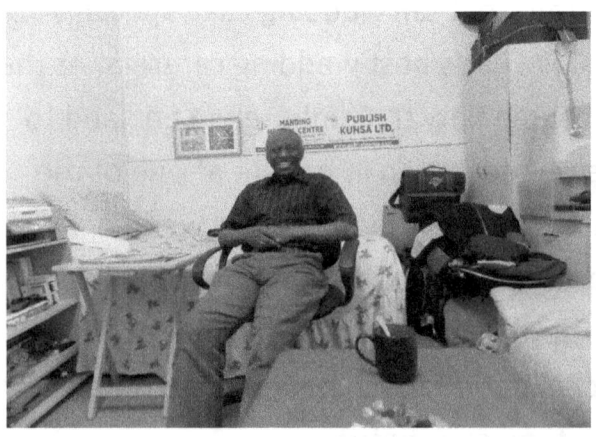

Dr. Ceesay on break from writing books

Chapter 11

ODES TO TENDER LOVING CARE: TLC

This Ode is dedicated to those who tirelessly gave themselves for the love of the other. A hungry peasant in the street given a piece of bread, a penny or a shilling makes his day and only caring love made the giver act in kind. Yes, the little acts of kindness we show are lives saving and it helps to give hope to others, especially the despondent and down trodden. Ignorance can at times be callous as demonstrated in the treatment of lepers in the olden days. Today a bit of TLC and medication allowed these to leave among society instead of spending the rest of their earthly life in dark caves and doomed dungeons. Carers of the aged, the sickly and disable deserve mention in being among the greatest golden hearts of our time. Bravo to all those gallant men and women who go to help in disaster zones, earth quakes, fire, or summanes catastrophes.

They do this out of love for you and I at the risk of their own very lives. I applaud wholeheartedly farmers who keep our breadbaskets filled, sailors who brave turbulent stormy oceans to get commerce moving, fishermen who challenge fires and angry seases to land a catch in other to provide us delicious fish meals, teachers who impart knowledge in us and all those bright minds that fly the metal bird to make global trotting lot easier than Christopher Colombo's days.

There is no greater TLC than it. Those with Alzheimer suffers can for sure attest to the dedication, patients, and love these unique people show as being fact of pure love for the self and others. No one can pay enough for the services of the housewife with husband and ten kids running around, Nurses, doctors, teachers, carers, police and even the solder.

What they give to society keeps all safe and informed for the day. They give safe TLC to allow us have restful nights like babies in slumber land and wake up to more TLC.

Dr. Alhasan Sisawo Ceesay, MD

Even young women can at times be overheard telling their friends that they intend to give tender loving care to their men when the men return from work. Yes, everyone needs and love TLC ala cart. Do not we feel great in the loving arms of our wives or lovers or mums? One should be thankful when someone else cares about us. Note the love and care a mother gives to her newly born. Nothing is greater TLC than maternal love and the eventual bonding that ensues between mother and child. Love makes us forgive and forget pain inflicted on us. Without TLC the world will be in endless storms. TLC is a charitable act that pervades all spheres of communities. TLC makes our hearts etched in others forever. TLC gives inspiration to the despondent and down trodden and it raises our spirits to higher heights. Hurray To TLC! Cheers my to my wife, and friends for loving me and for caring for both of us in this life. Tender loving care is phenomenon found in all higher mammals. Just watch documentaries about our cousins' monkeys, Apes, Gorillas, and Chimps and one would certainly note tender loving care being endlessly dispensed.

In the ghetto Tender Loving Care implies giving heart, soul, and feeling to the self and others. TLC magically transience gender and age. The old lady or man afraid of crossing the street would tell you relief he or she had from the gentle touch of a Scout or a police officer volunteering to help them cross to the other end of the street. It was all TLC in action and it leaves gratifying feeling for both giver and receiver.

"Always be my TLC." A true friend once sent this wish to me on my 50th birthday being a valentine day while I was in America. Hence we valentines do receive lot of cheers and TLC on our revered February 14th day of our lives.

It is normally said that business neither has a heart nor does it bleed but take it from me it does give TLC to its shareholders and governments that can dole millions if not billions of taxpayer's money to bail them for eating or spending in unsafe investments our invested monies within their world wide network of banks.

Dr. Alhasan Sisawo Ceesay, MD

TLC is strong feeling almost mystical in itself. I wish governments had the same heart or TLC to bail out ordinary folks like you and I from grips of unyielding joblessness, poverty and disease. Aids, Malaria, AK47dictocrats of the developing world, and rampant corruption are drowning mankind.

Where has the governments' TLC for man gone? We asked. TLC, TLC! My brothers and sisters bind us for good. At times I hear people moaning about the emptiness of life and turbulent waters it landed them. The urge to tell or ask if they ever tried the not so much of panacea TLC for it could just be the bridge they needed to get them over trouble waters of their lives.

Tender loving care to you and may TLC forever remain etched in our hearts. TLC is bounty wider than the Atlantic and deeper than any earthly ocean. The more we give ourselves to help others the more we receive from it. Like my valentine card, back in my student days in America yearned, I too ask readers to always give tender loving care to themselves and others. Cheers.

Njawara Banti Yassin

Chapter 12

BUSHLAND LOVE

Sare Toro Tayem is located in the woody area near the fringiest of the Dobo Forest some twenty miles from Manding Medical Center. At Njawara two doctors, Massembe Bah and Yoro Jalo shared a surgery for many years and had become the icon of private practice in the region. Nurse Adama Jange and Dr. Massembe were total strangers who now have to work at the Medical center at Njawara. Adam, a fully-qualified Staff Nurse, had leaved in Banjul, Gambia's capital, all her life and had never ventured or been to bush country nor did she ever come across Hyenas, Leopards, or seen life Antelopes roaming freely in mother nature's garden in the Savanna. Being city born she was frightened to death by crawling insects, snakes and lizards which undoubtedly will soon become among her regular guests' asides humans. None the less Nurse Adam Jange opted to follow her instinct and applied to work at the Manding Medical Centre three hundred miles in the hinter land. It was away from trappings of city life, neon lights, noisy motor cars and trucks plying to and fro to undefined destinations of commerce, restaurants and endless social amenities that she knew all her life but have to leave behind.

Dr. Massembe had decided to give her ride on his way back to the hospital at Manding Medical Centre in Njawara. In a jovial manner he asked her, "You do understand the danger in your decision?" Nurse Jange frowned at him making him feel embarrassed and thoughtless for trying to frighten the dickens out of a young lady determined to provide invaluable service to communities no other contemporary of her would want to go. In her mind she has her own questions about the air of mystery and charm that lurked in the man seating besides her asking silly boyish question and attempting to frighten her in other to have a conversation with her. She told him, "Do not worry for one of her uncles traded in Njawara for thirty years and spoke well of the people and the beauty of the Savanna." She told him lot of things had changed since his death. She broke off as a sob rose in her throat. After three years the memory of her adored uncle who had died suddenly and tragically in a road traffic accident in that same remote bush country, still brought painful tears to her eyes. Dr. Massebe let her know they will leave the next day. Her eyes shone with determination. She told him, "I want to go as soon as possible now that the Royal Victoria Hospital has released me there was no reason for any delay when there was so much to do in Njawara."

She added that she even have her personal luggage down to a toothbrush and a change of shirts and underwear ready. The next day at the arranged time Dr. Massembe arrived dressed as if heading to a VIP party. As he stepped out the van Nurse Jange looked round curious to see the stranger with whom she would soon be working so closely at the Manding Medical Centre in bush country.

He looked thirty some odd years she guessed. He was tall and fair, as most Fulanies, and his body was lean and muscular. His eyes weighed her up again but this time much more than the last time and his thin fulany lips in a solemn face relaxed into a faint smile in his attempt to maintain the doctor nurse protocol.

Nurse Adam Jange entered and sat at the passenger side while Dr. Massembe took to his driver's seat with Adam throwing or stealing a glance or two at his clean-shaven profile adorned with aroma of the best perfume there was at the time. He was certainly her ideal man and was very good looking she thought in silence.

Dr. Massembe broke the silence by telling Nurse Jange, "The Manding Medical Centre considers itself lucky to have her among its cadre of nurses. Your uncle worked so hard helping the villagers. We are delighted for your joining the team and they shook hands.

He reminded her of being told about the hardships that lie ahead at the Medical center."He told her the farmers and especially the children were suffering terribly from famine and disease and the countryside and the recent creeping of the Sahara desert in the Sahel region has devastated farms. From the sound of what he just said, Adam thought him to be a warm and compassionate man and she felt she would enjoy working with him.

She now kept wondering if this man was married. She chuckled at the thought that she was wondering about the private life of a stranger she just met for the first time. In flashed memory of the last paragraph in letter her uncle sent her before the accident came to her mind. "Dear Adam Jange, I have been busy lately as I had to send a convoy of food that was desperately needed by the villagers. The harvest had been poor this season. Sometimes we must do our best for these unfortunate farmers.

They do appreciate our effort in their behalf. If only there was more food, more medicines and supplies, and more medical personnel to help cope with the demand. Perhaps young boys and girls will join the medical profession and head to serve such places, as I am currently located."

It was that paragraph in the letter that helped her make up her mind about joining the medical center at Njawara. She had been thinking for some time of going out to her uncle and help in his work. Her father and mother died long ago when she was barely twelve years old, but throughout her childhood her uncle had been there for her. He even paid all her education and nursing training school fees and uniforms along buffered it with a fat monthly allowance.

The trip to Njawara would take almost three days drive over dusty bumpy roads but she was ready for the experience and would savor it to the fullest. "So sorry about your uncle Dr. Massebe said even though I never intended to revive emotions from you but just to strike a conversation over the long and tedious journey to Njawara". He now understood why she wanted to serve at the medical center at Njawara in bush land.

After four and half hours of dusty roads the vehicle stopped and Dr. Massembe escorted her to one of best of the best local Pasuar/ restaurants for a rest and delicious benechin commonly known as Jolof rice. It was only at this restaurant that the magic spells of woodland romance reared its head in their hearts. A beautiful sunset greeted them and smiling face of the staff added a décor to it all.

The place was clean and staff/girls not only appear immaculate but also were beautiful. Their smiles and winks made Adam Jange's heart percolate with jealousy for fear that the lovelies would steer her man away even though they were yet to be exposed. Clumsily she filled herself and had cocoa drink and pull a purse in attempt to pay for her share of the meal. At which time Dr. Massembe genteelly held hand and stopped her giving money to the waitress. He said, "Today is my turn for I know how you women libbers perceive men nowadays." This infuriated her but at the same time made her happy that he was not about to yield his machismo to a female with little money at hand.They took off and drove to Mansa konko where they each took different rooms at headquarters of the divisional commissioner for the night. Commissioner Tubab Davis treated them generously. The next day an early breakfast was prepared for them before they set off for next leg of the journey to Njawara. This time the two spoke freely and frequently while checking the social profiles of the other.Hence Nurse Adam Jange found that Dr. Massembe being a book worm never had chance to marry and had since returning from his medical training in the Uk settled at Njawara more concerned about plight of the villager little he could get out of social shoulder rubbing.

He does not hate women nor does he shun them but he just never made up his mind to be involved with any yet. He leaves alone in bungalow at the medical center. As for Nurse Adam Jange, she was born and breathes as city girl. Did all her schooling in Banjul. She did have the normal high school romances here and there but nothing serious nor was she ever involved with men since she took up nursing. She now heads to fulfill a long standing dream of hers, that is to carry the torch her uncle lit for the down trodden villagers. Every hour they spent seem to draw them closer as the veil of uncertain was gradually removed. Their next stop was at Janjanbure, a former home have returned slaves from America, now headquarters of Central Division. Again the commissioner matched the previous one at Mansa Konko in displaying hospitality to them. Again, they took different room but ate together seated side by side unlike at the restaurant. Lot of stories were heard from the commissioner about the area and of wild animals creeping into his bed room if the servants got careless to forget to luck the backs doors before darkness. By midnight the two visitors bide each other a good night full of sweet dreams and went straight for their designated rooms. This time sleep did not come easy to both of them as they started ruminating about the other and where does it all head to.

Would relationship materialized or was it a spur of the moment thing? Dr. Massembe was uncertain as to the fact that Nurse Adam Jange might just see another she falls for. He was going to take his time for as long as it need to be certain of her feeling for him with making any move or signaling his heart's yarning for her. Adam too was concern about his aloofness but happy that it kept him away from other ladies but that would not deter her archiving wining him over in due course. She did not feel like sleeping but afraid to walk out she stretched her feet at the corridor in the humidity of the night with bright skies and adorned by stars. There was constant humming of birds with strange creatures passing afar but she could not identify them. Looking further down the corridor she saw what looked like Dr. Massebe with some papers over deem light. At first she wanted to walk straight to him but that would make her look cheap and give him the upper edge of affairs. She held against her emotions and held her pride but did what most women do in trying to attention of a mate. She deliberately dropped the teacup she decided to pick up from her room to the corridor. Soon the watchman, the commissioner and of course the great doctor Masambe were at her side enquiring as to what went wrong and why was she not in bed that late of the night.

She turned away meaning to go back to her room but love overcame her and she plopped into the strong hands of the doctor. Both he and the commissioner took her to her bed and comforted her. She thank the men assured them se was ok but would like the doctor stay a while to keep an eye over her. She was not certain why she felt. Dr. Masembe got very worried and concern that she might be an epileptic or had some voodoo cast upon her by jealous competitor females. Whatever the case he was determined to get to the bottom of it before it become too late for both of them.

The others left after ten minutes leaving only Nurse Adam and DR. Massembe together in the room. She sprung to her feet as soon as she was certain that the others were sound asleep in their rooms and told Dr. Massembe that there was nothing wrong with her and that the whole affair was an act she did to call his attention but the noise from the teacup got out of proportion to draw the attention of the others for which she was sorry.

He understood and asked her not to apologies for he too could not sleep for the thought of her and their future. At that statement tears of joy dripped down the cheeks of Nurse Adam causing Dr. Massembe to uncontrollably lick them up clean from her face.

They embraced for the first time solemnly promising to keep each other forever and ever. "My love is yours forever", Dr. Massembe told the nurse clutched in his arms with him feeling her heart beat second by second. He set her to bed and left for his own room. Very soon the telephone rang and the two picked up where they left in conversation, which went through the wee hours of the night.

The commissioner was the first to visit sleepy Adam to find out how things went and whether she would need transport to take her back to the Royal Victoria hospital for further check up and examination. She assured him of no need for that and they would proceed to their destination, Manding Medical Centre. The host left a bit worried but relived knowing she was a nurse with a doctor in suitor.

Soon doctor and nurse were at breakfast throwing more romantic glances interwoven with smile that petrifies the beholder. They were both at cloud nine in their hearts as they have found each other and would try to keep it for life barring premature death. They took off and held hands throughout the rest of the journey with other warning of fears of loosing their grip.

After three days and almost twenty hours of dusty bumpy roads the van came to creaking stop at the bungalow of none other than Dr. Massembe. Children and caretakers of the place dashed to welcome him back. The kids told him how pleased they were for he had finally brought his wife with him. The girl said, "Welcome home mum and would you like coffee or tea and bread with it?" Adam Jange was not sure what to say but went along and said, "Yes if doctor will join me to a late mornings' cup of tea".

Dr. Massembe had his luggage unloaded from the van and he drove two streets away to Flat number 245 the new home of Nurse Adam Jange. Alas! She made it to Njawara. More than any thing is she looked forward to meeting the hospital administrators and getting acquainted with the wards, patients, staff and not the least residents of Njawara.

She spruced up and looked at her pretty face while accidentally speaking to the mirror for a while. She finally threw herself to the bed for a few minutes relaxation after such long and tiring journey to Njawara. She tried to close her eyes but the images of Massembe would not leave her free. She went to the already supplied kitchen and poured herself some milk in warm chocolate and drank it slowly.

She turned the FM Radio and had familiar voices of the Banjul theatre. Right then she felt home sick and asked if her resignation from the Royal Victoria Hospital was not premature and spur of the moment decision. She finally concluded that it was too late to change her mind and besides she wanted to do work like this for the down trodden and no place deserve her service.

Also a bonus in the form of Dr. Messembe was now certain for her. Only a fool would turn her back from such opportunity to serve and be loved inclusively. It was not until after six pm did Dr. Massembe called to check on her and told her that he decided to give her few moments for rest and reflection.

She was happy to hear him and the conversation went on for hours as if they were teenagers not known when to hang up the phone. He cautioned her that they must move slowly to avoid rumormongers etc. She retorted and asked if he was hiding from a girl friend in the region. Dr. Massembe emphasized that the tradition of the region is different from big city Banjul and that he wants people to respect her and not see her as a swinger. She understood about concerns he expressed and promised not to go off guard. They then had a long goodbye kiss and retired for the night.

Njawara Banti Yassin

The first thing Nurse Adam noticed was the braying of the donkeys intermingled with sporadic howls of hyenas. This scared the dickens out of her and made her first night away from big city Banjul traumatic. She hardly slept for fear that these animals will jump through her window and have her as a rare snack. It was almost dawn orchestrated by the sounds of cocks all over the village. She could not wait for day brake to tell Dr. Massembe of her first night at Njawara.

She had her breakfast and headed for the admin building to meet Matron Ramatulie Jarala Ceesay. Ram as the staff knew her, was a cheerful cheery individual who welcomed Nurse Adam. After a brief chat they headed to the wards for Adam to meet the staff and see things in reality at Manding Medical Centre.

Sister Jainaba, the in-charge of Female Surgical was the first they met. There was a warm handshake and welcome to Female surgical. They walked through and as they pass patients Adam thought, without saying it loud, that there was so much to do for the patients manned by so skeletal a staff number. Some of the younger male patients watched with interest as she went from bed to bed. These sceneries were repeated throughout the hospital complex and ancillary units.

She was overwhelmed by the cheerfulness and hard working staff she met. Things were not like that at her ward at the Royal Victoria Hospital in Banjul where she worked since becoming a nurse. She loved the atmosphere and team spirit of her new place. Manding Medical Centre was good choice and place to work indeed.

On returning to Matron's office she was given the regular uniform of the hospital and asked to take the rest of the weekend off to familiarize herself with Njawara and the shops. She starts duty at the Pediatrics ward on Monday. She was delighted for her love of children made her specialized in pediatric nursing.

No sooner than reaching her flat did she call Dr. Massembe, enquired about his day, asked if he missed her and spilled the beans of being very happy that she came and that she was much impressed by the staff and cleanliness of the hospital in general. She was looking forward to start at the Pediatric ward on Monday.

Doctor Massembe summarized his day as being very hectic with lot of surgical cases and that the male surgical ran out of beds. Unlike Banjul, which has mixed wards, Manding Medical Centre prides itself in keeping the genders apart for respectability and comfort of the patient.

This was another aspect that Adam noticed and liked about her new hospital. Despite the rush of things he did miss being by her side etc. He invited her to dine with him at his Bungalow after 7 pm, which she accepted unhesitatingly for she was itching to be kissed by his sweet lips once more. The table was set for two by the time she arrived.

A bouquet of bougainvilleas flowers welcomed her at the door and after jointly listening and watching the evening news the couple migrated to the dinning table to fill themselves with delicious Domoda and Njar Meu drinks. Neither of them partake alcohol or spirits but coca cola and Fantail took waves. Having filled their Tommies they moved to the couch and watched video drama plays, in each other's arms, by Senegalese, Gambian and Nigerian artists until well after midnight before she retired to her flat very happy indeed.

She revels in these dramas on local daily chitchats and romantic stories. The visit ended at midnight for Doctor. Massembe has a full schedule of operations, which start 7:00 Am prompt. They said goodbye and she went home very elated. For some reason the sounds of the night never border her as it did in her first night. Hence, she slept soundly like a log until 9:00 Am when the made showed up to clean the flat.

The next day being Saturday, she got up late and had a quick bath and breakfast to allow the young lady do her daily chores. She then took a walk to main town Njawara's shopping center. You guessed it. She stole the show for being the new tantalizing girl in the block. She had so much attention she never bargained for. Men and elderly women praised her for coming to help and even expressed admiration of her petrifying beauty.

Her presence sent jitters into hearts of young ladies who feared loosing their men to her for she was a magnet to men. Having seen most of the shopping malls and done her own bit of shopping, she walked away from the metropolitan sector of Njawara. Soon she reached collections of mud huts built about in open space with no fencing around them. Smoke bellowing from half a dozen huts rose lazily into the still hot air. A dozen or so of women and children eyed her as she finds her way around the huts.

A little boy of four, sucking his thumb, walked by her. He smiled and held her hand and said, "Welcome to our village miss." He had huge red eyes in a sunken face with pathetically thin arms staring at her. Nurse Adam Jange asked herself if they were all this malnourished. The boy's legs seem hardly able to support his swollen potbelly.

At the end tears welled from nurse' eyes. She had heard of stories of hunger in the region but never dreamt it to be this devastating. The sight of the little boy gave her more resolve strength to work at the pediatric ward for the rest of her life or stay at Mamding Medical Centre. She would contact international agents and UNESCO for relief in their behalf and she vowed to work to help these beleaguered children.

Dr. Massembe was more than delighted to hear her reaction to the plight and need for help in the region and promised to do all he could to let the chief executive bless her projects for the region's children. Both Doctor and nurse spent most of the day indoor at their residents. Doctor was finalizing lecture he was to deliver to the medical students doing their electives at Manding Medical Centre and nurse had decided to take it easy and take in the change that met her since leaving big city Banjul.

They spoke briefly over the phone and then let the rest of the day find its path. Monday marked the first day of duty at the pediatric ward for Nurse Jange. She arrived twenty minutes early and made good impressions on the sister on duty who was happy about her. She greeted everyone and along with the rest of the staff took over the ward from the night team.

Dr. Alhasan Sisawo Ceesay, MD

It all went smoothly for its repetition of her daily life at the Royal Victoria Hospital in Banjul. The junior staff and auxiliaries loved her simplicity and ability to lead without being implosive. The young doctors started showing interest, just as Dr. Massembe feared and had cautioned her on their way to Njawara. Nonetheless she stuck to her guns and had the young bulls follow hospital protocol and not think they can muscle their way to her heart. She has her eyes and heart already set on Dr. Massembe and would not exchange him for any infatuated male doctor period. No wonder then the first question coming from Dr. Massembe asked about the young doctor's behavior toward her. She assured him of having put them in their rightful places and that he; Dr. Massembe was her idol and love. That will not change for any reason other death separating them. Hearing this much commitment from her pleased doctor Massembe and it boosted his confidence to match forward with head held high. He too reaffirms his undying love for her and promised to marry her as soon as she gets her feet on the ground at Manding Medical Centre. Nurse Adam did exactly what she resolved. Much aid came to the village from various churches and UN organization since the first encounter with potbelly boy at the outskirts of Njawara.

In the wards her work had been superb and lots of good confidential reports and recommendation both from parent of children, nurses and doctors who worked with her, were sent to her file at the Matron's office. It was to no one's surprise of her being automatically nominated to take over the pediatric ward when the current in-charged retire on health grounds.

She became head nurse at the Manding Medical centre's pediatric unit two years after joining the hospital staff. This was rapid promotion indeed and she and Dr. Massembe savoured it very well. She found Dr. Massembe very helpful indeed but wished her uncle were alive to witness her contributions.

In silence, at her flat, she raised a glass full of milk and said, "Uncle this one is for you. Rest happily and know that your torch shall continue to light the path of these people who are touched by its generousness. Cheers!" Both the district authority and Governor of the region gave awards for job well done and encouraged her to teach other ladies in the Nursing field.

Dr. Massembe's parents hail from Kerr Ado a stone throw from Njawara. His father migrated to Banjul in search of greener pastures. He eventually met and instantly fell in love with Kumba Mokalpoch of Kerr Willan in Dingare ward, Banjul and married her.

Dr. Alhasan Sisdawo Ceesay, MD

They had Massembe and two other girls. Now Dr. Massembe had return to his father's native land to provide a much needed medical service to the region. Today he is going to fulfill his father's wish that is to marry and present him a grandchild before he joins God and their ancestors in heaven. He invited Nurse Adam to his Bungalow and to her greatest surprise, even though she knew he would propose but this day took her by surprised. Hence, after their normal formalities, Dr. Massembe took out a small box and another full of beautiful dresses specially made for Adam and said, "This is for you. I love you and want you be my wife for life." Adam quickly opened the first small box wrapped with colors of the Gambia and found a pure gold ring in it. Overwhelmed she said, "Yes, I love you and would be the happiest girl in the block being your wife and mother of your children. May God anion our wish for happiness, health and prosperity together." They kissed again and again as if that was their first in life. He followed tradition by sending his uncles and close friend to approach parents of Adam Jange for her hand in marriage. The delegation came back with the proposal being accepted and that the Imam, their parents and elders of Banjul will be offering prayers to officially sanction the marriage between them at the Grand Banjul Mosque the following week.

Njawara Banti Yassin

Dr. Massembe drove to Banjul to attend the occasion. Mean while both staff of the Manding medical center, Njawara and all nearby district went into a massive preparation for the wedding ceremony of the cherished nurse and doctor they ever had. All sorts of presents of ladies embroidery some set aside animals they would donate for slaughter for food during the ceremony. The semi wealthy bought diamond studded necklaces, gold bangles with matching earrings. The cobblers made special ancient but well decorated pairs of shoes for the bride. The grand day came a month after Dr. Massembe announced that their intending to marriage. Tribes from the region and afar poured in not only to participate but also to show their gratitude to the couple and also witness another unique occasion for the region. It was rare thing for Banjul born to shorn the glitter of Banjul and have their historic moment celebrated in bush country, So everyone was elated and danced to their heart's content in marking the true meaning of the day for the couple and celebrants. It was a cheerful and memorable day that none of them would ever forget. The drums, dancing, chanting of scribes was spectacular. The bride and bridegroom were overwhelmed with bundles upon bundles of presents and animals lined up for slaughter in their behalf.

The hospital staff did not lag behind in showing appreciation and generosity to the colleagues in wedding. None other than the chief executive, matron and the governor of entire region, presented special gifts from the hospital. This then was community in action and display of gratitude and ineptness for kindness shown to the by the couple.

The Governor of the region gave long speeches as what an exemplary thing these couple had been to them all. He praised them over and over and wished them happiness in their lives together. It was a joyous occation for all he concluded. The region's representative follows with similar line of comments and again paid for the pair's happiness.

The mayor of Njawara spoke in behalf of the villagers and pointed out the impact Nurse Adam Jange and Dr. Massembe had on the life of the villagers especially the children who she worked so hard to have international and UN agents come to their aid. He was personally indebted to them eternally and would name his next child after Adam if a girl or Dr. Massembe if it urn out to be a male. Everyone laughed but understood the significant of it. It was an honour bestrode to a few for such a remarkable Mayor to name one of his after an individual.

The ceremony went on until late at night before the celebrants retired to bed. The next day the couple flew to America for a two months holiday.

They returned to their jobs two months late but with Adam carrying triplets for Dr. Massembe. She refused maternity leave until two weeks to her due day before taking rest to prepared for the arrival of the babies. Her instinct for call of nursing dwarfs that of most people.

Mrs. Famatanding Ceesay-Mballow, Daughter

Dr. Alhasan Sisawo Ceesay, MD

Chapter 13

DESERT LOVE'S ALIBI

Muntu Tabal is a young Bedouin girl who tends camels on the fringes of the mighty Sahara Desert. With her we will be walking across mounds of endless sand dunes and be pelted with thirty to sixty miles per hour winds of pebble cum sand. The alibi you are about to discover is nothing less than pure love and endearment shrouded with unheard of tenacity. A passionate affair leads Ali Ben Bella to Muntu. Ali and Muntu's Bedouin ancestors had once wandered as far field as Libya and Tunis in time tiring of the nomadic life. Her tribe's men would meet at the palm fringes or the outskirts of an Oasis where other Bedouins and merchants had gathered to join a caravan.

Baggage loaded camels set off after morning prayers. Over the next days, weeks, and even months they progress slowly through the desert on southeasterly tract camping at night and traveling through the day. A well-marked trail of wells helped them on their way, and all along the route they pass caravans traveling in the opposite direction making the barren and inhospitable wastes animated and safe.At some distance a well surfaces. Here they try a short rest with refreshments and letting the animals drink before proceeding.

Many other caravans join in carrying gold, salt, and other fanciful goods. It would be long, torturous journey only eased by the use of tents made out of camel wool and skin with supporting frames. They play chess and other simple games to minimize boredom, while traveling through fierce inhospitable desert. They would offload at a trading center and redirect their camels for another caravan trip. The circle repeats over and over through the years of a Bedouin's life.

Ali's father had remarkable skill in curing the sick and was knowledgeable in the art of healing. He had acquired reputation as healer, besides herding camels, who could do miracles with his desert herbs and roots. Patients came from all over the surrounding caravans and hamlets of tents villages, and at one time he had been much sought after for his opinions on herbal medicine. Now Muntu and Ali never met until in one of his father's healing field days that the two met and fell in love instantly.

In Bedouin society, it was dangerous to have fiancé but Muntu would rather face death than not see Ali Ben Belle. Young men and women being forbidden to mingle made Muntu contrived a simple deceptive female dress for her Ali. It was a hooded dress with just slights or small holes for the eyes.

Ali Ben Belle was in addition gifted ventriloquist and sounded more like a girl than any would imagine in that dark robed gown provided by Muntu Tabal. They now at least have perfect camouflage but the rendezvous became a thorn in their burnets. Watchful eyes scan movement of ladies in almost all their wakeful lives. Muntu did not tell any of her friends, even the most trusted ones, for fear of being prematurely revealed because of jealousy. Ali was also not about to let the cat out of the bag.

The desert sheep became their only salvation and acceptable means of being away from normal crowds and be together alone. Hence both took great interest in taking their camels to oasis to fetch water and bring some dates to their families. This routine made their parents comfortable and happy unknown to them that Muntu and Ali meet at far away oasis, risking their lives should a rapid sand storm imaged.

Muntu was in her sweet sixteen years of life while Ali in his tender nineteen years old. They were so enamored that fear of the penalty of death if caught never ran into their minds. All they plot for and yearn was to meet in oasis love, eat dates, drink fresh water and camel milk and sleep awhile in each other's arms after kissing and endless vigorous sex.

This went on for months on end and one fine day Muntu found her getting dizzy and vomiting on getting out of bed. Worst she started craving for food she never liked before then she would wonder from tent to tent looking for fruits hardly available in Bedouin Dom. Her weight accelerated which at first her elder sister, Hanna Tabal, only noticed. It occurred only because the two had shared beddings and tents since their early days. Neither kept anything away or hidden from the other. Except in this for Muntu never told Hanna that she was involved with Ali Ben Belle. Ali would be hanged at dawn should it come out that he was having an illicit affair with Muntu. Bedouins take their culture and formalities of marriage very seriously and no mitigating circumstances would be accepted should a culprit be caught. No sex until after marriage ceremony applies to both sexes without ifs and buts about penalty to be levied upon infractions. Next to notice change in Muntu was none other than the desert scout and camel rider, Mahmud, who by the way saw them several times heading to the oasis love but thought them to be two women. He was not by Bedouin law allowed to be close enough for fear of infringing in their rest and privacy. However on his last encounter he was able to hear a distinct male voice, which reverted to that of female voice when his presence was noticed.

Mahmud just greeted them in Bedouin style and continued to another well far from where Muntu and Ali rendezvoused. The scene however stuck in his memory so much so that the day he saw Muntu expanding and behaving out of the normal he sent alarm bells without it seeming like he knew or was orchestrating it. At first impulse he thought it duty to tell Muntu's parents what he found out but there was the dark chance of being accused of being the culprit as the two would still be considered innocent teenagers smeared by a desert bandit. Mahmud was in his young days one of those who had terrible history regarding women and history has it that he was once saved from lynching by a young lady he raped. Above all he was certain that Muntu would not hesitate to swear that he, Mahmud, made her pregnant and threatened to kill her should she tell. She would even say they met on several occasions behind some calm but hidden surroundings where he seduced her and had sex with her many times a week. His bad reputation versus tears pouring out of seemingly innocent Muntu would convince angels to agree with Muntu's version of the tale. Having had this scenario run over and over in his head he concluded it best to leave dying dogs lye still and never uttered a word about his findings to any one else.

Soon Muntu would not remove the long dress when with the other girls in the tent. They teased her as being Fatima, wife of a pious priest of yester years. It was her vomiting and weight gain that alerted Muntu's mother to call her to a Tate a tote between only mother and daughter.

In Bedouin tradition mothers are tried for miss behaviors of their daughters especially if these became pregnant out of wedlock. So mom wanted to know the truth and what, where and who was the male culprit before she becomes sacrificial lamb for crime she knew nothing about. Muntus form changed and experienced old ladies had started teasing her mom about possibility of Muntu being a woman about to welcome a stranger within the Tabal family. At first Muntu's mother frowned at the thought that her daughter was pregnant with an illegitimate child for an unknown male. So she promised to get to the bottom of it once and for all by having a chat with Muntu.

Not knowing that Muntu and Ali had planned to elope the same time she was to meet her mother should their cover be exposed. Muntu and her mother each took a camel and headed for the sand dunes away from inquisitive ears. Ali Ben Belle followed at a distance not to be noticed by Muntu's mom.

Mother and daughter stopped at a well where they were supposed to be alone and let go of the animals to drink and rest. While sharing fresh dates Muntu's mother opened up the Pandora's box by letting the cat out of the bag. She simply said, Muntu you know you are one of my dearest daughters and am certain you would not want both of us killed for something we can solve right away. Muntu's eyes opened widely in fear for she has had of mothers who killed their daughters for staining the family's name and honor. Yet she asked her mother at what was she alluding at about her that would resort to their death? She assured Muntu of her motherly love and urged her calm down and come clean to mom. Mom in tears told Muntu how the tents are riff with rumor that she was pregnant and it would prove out in six months time. Why did she choose to disgrace the Tabals linage? She lamented the grievous error her draught entangled with a Bedouin boy of the like of Ali Ben Belle. Tale now exposed made both more fearful of the repercussions from the tribe would be. It is believed that no Bedouin daughter dose things like that behind their mothers. She then and therein pulled a knife and just as she was about to thrust it into her own heart Ali stepped in and took the knife incurring a slight cut in the struggle. Ali apologized and told her that Muntu was his life and without her he would rather die than live one second longer.

He told Muntu's mom that the forces of love in his heart for Muntu lead to their act. They will take off to Mauritania and would send messages and presents with photos of their newborn when they eventually settle in that desert country of southern Sarah. The trio prayed, hugged and kissed several times. Ali was then able to talk mom into agreeing upon the only alibi left to the couple before the public proof of the pregnancy. Mother and daughter were to return and be seen to have entered the tents among other women. Later that evening Muntu was to step out quietly to allow hatching up one of the greatest Bedouin elope stories of the century. This way both will be free of any possible charges of infidelity or misguiding one's child. Even then Muntu and Ali risk being lost in the desert for they dare not follow normal caravan routes. They would be tracked by the Sahara's best riders should her disappearance come to light quicker than anticipated. But go Muntu must at the tender age of seventeen because that was the only way to safe the lives of her lover and mother. The two lovers met at the appointed time and place, loaded their camels from stuff they kept and headed deep South towards Mauritania while mom watched until the figures merged with the desert and blue skies. Mom returned home but dare not tell her husband about what she now knew nor was it safe for the eloped might be tracked out.

Her husband being an impulsive man would lunch a public search team after Ali's head. It would be Ali's parents who eventually set the alarm bells after not seeing him for more than a fortnight. Friends told of having seen him tending camels just before dawn two weeks ago. They believe he must have been lost in the desert. Some put two and two together and came up with the possibility that he Ali might have something to do with the mysterious simultaneous disappearance of the Tabal girl whose father is up in arms about her. Hence, a search team of the best riders and scouts was mobilized and sent out to seek the kids but these had to return without a trace of the Ali and Muntu. The old man of the oasis let word that Ali's parents should confide with Muntus' mother at the next encampment five miles away. This was done and to their segrin Muntu and Ali had some common disappearing days. So the elders of the two camps met and had candid discussion and also received explanation to the possibility of an eloped hatched by Ali and Muntu. Council turned to Muntu's mother and in harsh manner commanded her to tell all she knew, if not she would suffer full force of the law when the truth surfaces. Scared of death but determined to protect her daughter, she told the gathering that the last time she saw Muntu was when they went together to fetch dates.

Her daughter insisted on searching for better ones
located far into the desert near Betel, which tale council
accepts as safe for children of her age. It would be now
three days since she; her husband and his brother rode to
Betel and found no trace of Muntu or Ali. Not even the
dates Muntu was collecting were found. She too, like Ali's
father fear fowl play from bandits of the desert. She wept
at the end of her statement, what tantamount to
crocodile tears for among all she knew exactly what
happened where the kids are headed. Some believed her
while others had their doubts and demanded more from
her. They asked if she knew that her daughter might be
pregnant, as rumor of such development had been
circulating the camps. She, with head low replied in the
negative and inferred that was the first time she heard
about such a nonsense smearing her daughter's
character.Then the old man of the oasis was asked to
step forward and tell all he knew about relationship
between Ali and Muntu. He started by telling the
gathering that it was a week ago, past noon, when he
was at the oasis love and there he met or noticed two in
women dresses but one was male for he had no female
intonations. The voice was all male. He even went as
close as could be to try to identify the person but the veil
concealed his identity.

He told council that when he heard Ali speak at the camp it left him with no doubts that the voice was the same he had heard the other day at the oasis of love. Asked why he failed to alert the community. He said it was a mistake predicated on dark history his life had when he was a young man in which instant a woman who he raped prevented him being lynched. Muntus' mother denied every word said by the old man and obviously tried to brand him as an accomplished in the disappearance of the kids. To prove her point she begged to illustrate her point by asking two well-veiled people in the crowd to come forward and speak and then for the old man to identify which was male or female. The old man was threatened with facing the gallows if he were found to have a hand in the saga. For a moment he blamed himself for spilling some of the beans out without a witness to support his version about Muntu and Ali. However he believed that the truth will one-day surface to vindicate him for it never lags behind the righteous. He took heart and challenged Muntus' mom to swore that she was not present and advisor to the possible eloping of her pregnant daughter with Ali Ben Belle to South of the Sahara in an effort to safe her own neck and shame it brings to the Tabal family.

The gathering went silent but female ingenuity surfaced and the old man faltered at identifying voices he purportedly heard at the oasis of love. The revelation sent jitters into Muntus mom's heart for if she told the truth she would be hanged and her daughter would also in the end be killed and so would be the fate of Ali, who she now likes very much as son in law. Hence she prayed for God to give her the right words of utterance in this challenging crowd poised to lynch both she and her daughter and grandchild if found. She reminded the council how the old man had just demonstrated how wrong he could be and that he conjured the scenario to free his neck from the gallows. She swore of being innocent of knowing about her daughter meeting with Ali or their disappearance being planned. She like any and all mothers only prays that their children are alive and safe some where from heavy sand storms in the desert or south of the Sahara. The way she delivered her plea of innocence and tenacity made council to accept her version and freed her of criminal neglect or charges.At the end no one believed the old man of the oasis.He choused the woman as male and had to run away in shame. This trick was what let Muntus' mother off the hook. At first Ali's father swore that his son was the best Bedouin boy in the whole of the desert and had nothing to do with disappearance of the Tabal girl.

Dr. Alhasan Sisawo Ceesay, MD

He suggested the possibility of slave riders having kidnapped their children and being the culprits behind their current lost bereavement. He suggested they check the coastal region of Senegal and Gambia River valley. Being a respected elderly man council believed him and had the case closed at that point by agreeing to send word to bother Gambia and Senegal in an effort to locate Muntu and Ali.

Council agreed to send a second wave of expert trackers as far as Mauritania and Senegal. Muntus father never testified demonstrating Bedouin chauvinism. So all able-bodied men took to the saddle and bit their goodbye and headed for the desert and south of the Sarah in search of illusive lost kids in love.

Three separate teams were set one headed south and the other as Far East as the desert allows the expedition. With the third heading for Algeria and Tunis frequent caravan stopping trade centers of the day. Everyone wished them God's guidance and safe return to his or her family. All three-search groups returned without a trace of Ali or Muntu. Worst, they never even heard news of what might have happened to them. Nonetheless some of the search party decided to stay in Mauritania and raised families there than return to the hash life of nomadic Bedouins.

Those who stayed long enough in Senegal did come across a couple similar to the one they set out after some years ago but could not fully identify them as Ali and Muntu even though some doubt lingered in their mind about the sighting. Only, Fatim, Muntus' mom, knew the truth which if revealed at the time would spell doom for her, Muntu and Ali.

Bedouin law was ruthless if not merciless towards those breaking it as it is used without compassion towards the guilty. Rulings of the council are irreversible and sentences are summarily carried out as soon as the judge decreed it. Desert life was hard and these rulings were meant to protect property, women, children and the elderly from marauders.

There was no concept of mitigating circumstances for consideration by the judge. Nor was there idea of a possible miss carriage of justice or fresh evidence being available to warrant retrial after decision had been taken on a case. The Bedouins were knowledgeable groups who traveled length and breath of the Sahara desert gaining experience and education about it has terrains. They were not born to privilege or entitlement and were neither aristocrats nor solders per say.

The vast majority were camel herding and transporters of goods across rugged terrain of the Sahara to dusty market towns along its fringes. A few became wealthy but were not by any means, amongst the most powerful camel traders of their time. Most were small caravans running small family affairs and businesses.

Those who eventually settled in Senegal and Mauritania were, despite there generally modest circumstances were endowed with a respectable level of education and few became among the most learned scholars of their day. Mean while Muntu and Ali had made it safely to Mauritania but decided to proceed further to Senegal in avoidance of trackers and caravans that might locate them prematurely.

They now abandoned desert life in favor of settling in Senegal. They changed their names knowing that search teams would use it in trying to locate their where about. Muntus mother was advancing in age. When one day a lady in dark dress stepped quietly into her chamber in the tent and after the greeting formalities told her that she hails from Maracas and has a special parcel from Muntu Tabal and Ali Ben Belle for her. Muntus' mother could neither believe her ears nor her sight of the parcel being gently handed to her wrapped with decorated paper.

She kissed the visitor several times and dance around for sight of someone who can proof that her daughter escaped the volcanic jaws and cruel sand storms of the Sahara Desert. In the parcel were six photos: two of her grandson, one of Ali and Muntu separately and one with the two together kissing happily.

The sixth photo was the recent addition to the family, a baby girl that was named after Muntus mother, Fatima. In addition there were lots of other gifts in the big parcel but the photos were the most cherished. They brought life and hope back to Muntus' mother's heart. Both women were so moved that they wept in joy for the good news and the messenger left hurriedly before being noticed by men returning from prayers.

The news of Muntu being safe brought a miraculous recovery for Fatima. However, like before she kept everything in her heart. The messenger returned to Maracas unnoticed and told Ali and Muntu the mission was accomplished without a hitch and that his parents were well but constantly praying for their well being and happiness intermingled with prosperity. Muntu tried to squeeze out every bit of information she could get about her dear mother Fatima and Sister Hanna. She asked about her health, aging and impact her eloping had on the family.

All their fears were allayed by the returning lady who did her best to calm and reassure Muntu that all is well except that everyone misses her and Ali. It left Muntu elated and energized. Many more presents, parcels and photos of themselves and the children were sent secretly many times over the years. It would be fifteen years since the coupled eloped before Muntu and Ali would venture to visit their aging and sick parents since revealing their where about.

For the visit they had loads of presents for nearly every member of the Klan and much more ready for both families. In addition they took a thousand of the best breeds of Arabian camels with them for their parents to share. It took them almost two months travel across sand dunes and heated wind and sand storms to rendezvous with their nomadic families near Al Ashra Oasis.

The height of dust raised by camel hoofs made the entire encampments come out to witness the arrival of an Arabian prince or reagent. Only this time it was surprisingly and delightfully one of them who was long given up for being casualty of the raging sands of the Sahara Desert. Ali and his twelve-year-old son Mustapha helped by Muntu and their six-year-old daughter Fatima drove the thousand camels.

The spectators were more than happy and amazed at how Ali managed such large group of unruly camels across hash terrain of the desert. First, on arriving, Ali had the camels herded then embanked upon Bedouin tradition by walking straight to his aging in-laws, apologized and declared himself husband of Muntu Tabal after gaining their blessings. He then returned to Muntu and told her the good news allowing them to be reunited with their parents and Klan. He told her that a date had been selected by their parents for their formal weeding ceremony to take place in a month's time. One now wonders what were the reactions of all those who threatened to kill Muntu's mom, Ali and Muntu herself for disappearing into thin air fifteen years ago. Fatim, Muntu's mom kept her secret about Ali and Muntu until the day the couple and caravan of a thousand camels arrived at their tent. Ali gave camels, gold and lots of dressings as dowry for Muntus' hand in marriage which her parents gladly accepted and announced their weeding to mark the joyous return of Ali and Muntu. They were very happy to be blessed with three grand children since their eloping fifteen years ago. As for Fatima, Muntu' mom and Ali' mom Lala they decided to have the biggest wedding ceremony in thanking all those who stood by them during the unexplained disappearance of Ali and Muntu.

Hence they managed to convince Ali and Muntu to have a proper Bedouin tribal marriage ceremony before returning to Senegal. In Bedouin Dom parents and relatives would wish for nothing less or better since a marriage between first cousins, the child of a brother, was traditionally regarded as an ideal sort of union; a strengthening of an already existing bond between Ali's father and Muntu' father. By it the labyrinth of relationships are guarded and passed onto other generations. A date was set and an announcement and invitation to attend the festivity of it went to all camps and tent as far as a camel can cover in a day. And rider's eye can see. For weeks on end, Bedouin tribes with wealth poured in their gifts, which ranged from gold, trinkets and diamond necklaces, camels, goats, sheep, goats, and special colored camel skin and wool tents. Every thing connotes festivity fit for Sheiks or Arab royalty. A fair weather day was chosen for the wedding ceremony. Prayer consummated the marriage followed by lots of people coming around Ali's tent, all the young men and girls singing and dancing without care in their world. The bride's father provided lot of food and fruits to be had along with camel milk and even fruit juice from Tunis. Supper consisted of lamb, camel meat, rice, and sweetened meat standing on matted floor and tables.

Friends and relatives joined the festivity during the day and again in the evening to dance and sing to their hearts' content. Some sat in the tent while a large crowd gathers in the open; there were at least three hundred boys and girls packed in semicircle in front of the bride and groom. The newly wed couples were sitting on mat enthroned with their backs against the tent, while their friends and relatives dance and chant. Ali, the groom, was a dark sturdy young man smiling most of the time. He was dressed in new gowns of golden color. Muntu wore a white gown, with a trill of lace and gauze veil. Her face and hands were carefully painted decoratively to match the class and situation. It made her radiant. It was well past sunset and faces around the bridal couple glowing under a dome of golden dust in the light of kerosene lamps. The drumming beat was measured and gentle until upon entry of a girl into the center with beautiful dress and long scarf tied around her waist started dancing with both hands on her hips. Dancing with eyes fixed to the newly wed, she moved her hips at first with slow graceful gyrations, then backwards and forwards with the rest of her body staying still; almost immobile, except for the quick circular motion of her feet. Then gradually, almost undetectable, the tempo of the drumbeat quickened followed by chants upon chants by the crowd.

They clap loudly and the girl in the center raised her hand and pointed to her head in a graceful arc. Her body again turning and rotating slowly in one place with hips moving faster while the crowd clapped and stamped their feet amid roaring approval at the top of their voices. The faster the drumbeat the faster the girl gyrates to the astonishment of the crowd. A boy stepped in the center but could not march the girl's magical movement. In the end all thronged around, danced, clapping and chanting, intoxicated with the heightened eroticism of the wedding night full of feverish air and mysteries of the heart. These scenes were repeated by various groups of dancers for another three days with talk of décor and dress of the bride and his groom. Many wished their children's day be as fabulous as Ali's if not better but not lesser quality and popularity. When time came for Ali and Muntu to return to Senegal, they decided to leave their twelve-year-old son, Mustapha, with their parents for him to learn about his culture and values it pride itself. He would join them when he reaches twenty before the expiration of his Senegalese passport. Multitudes lined part of the route when Muntu and Ali bit the Klan goodbye and headed for Senegal this time as legitimate husband and wife leaving happy parents, Klan and relatives continue their Bedouin life as practiced by their ancestors since the beginning of time.

Njawara Banti Yassin

Chapter 14

ROWAN & SIBILA, JOYOUS UNION OF HEARTS

When their mould was completed the two had unique similarities and philosophy towards life. They are very kind and friendly. Both are committed to helping people. Sibila, Portugal's beauty at heart and face is a solicitor by vocation and Rowan Sheddon-Harvey, my Brit, is a businessman and an agent in the travel industry. He works at the Skynet Travel Company at Wilmslow Road in Manchester. Coming to know these young would soon be couples made me feel blessed being their friend. Let us first start at the beginning when I casually met Rowan Harvey-Sheden around Christmas time in 2004 while engaged at the Punjab Collection Clothing and Shoe shop at 225 Wilmslow Road in Manchester. We used to chat for long covering various topics ranging from politics, world affairs and down to simple daily experiences and our desire to help bring relief to some of these nightmares. Our commonality of objectives in this life made it even easier for us to become inseparable brothers. Rowan visited me at 225 Great Western Street in Moside frequently bring food for us to share. He was the first Brit to get me out of my den and have some food at a restaurant. Until then I do not venture going tout for lack of money and being engrossed in my studies.

He enjoyed reading my works (books) and wonders at the speed and rate with which I can produce a completed manuscript. Very soon Rowan became conversant with work or my efforts to provide medical aid to Gambian villagers. In reality he felt sad and sorry for me because of the unfortunate way life turned out for me in the United Kingdom. He said, Ceesay it is so pathetically sad that you found your-self at a Clothing and Shoe shop instead of being at a hospital treating patients. Rowan was so moved by my determination and goal for the villager that he and Zia Haque of Skynet Travel Company contributed more than five hundred pounds sterling towards the building of the children's unit of the Manding Medical Centre at Njawara village, the Gambia, West Africa. While at the Punjab Collections trying to make ends meet Rowan was kind enough to assist with another five hundred for me settle my rent and utility bills. In addition back in August 2008 he came to my rescuer with a loan of two hundred and fifty pounds sterling to help keep my daughters in school in the Gambia. He said, Ceesay, pay me as soon as you can and hope you would be able to sort-out your life soon. Among his many acts of kindness is that he never stopped checking on me or inviting me to spend a day or two at his Flat.

In addition he recently donated two computers for use at the Manding Medical Centre. In a nutshell Rowan is my British Samaritan and brother. Beautiful Sibila is a devoted Catholic committed to helping the needy. I met her with Rowan in 2007 while distributing door-to-door advertisement leaflets for Taxi Company. Right then I knew some thing magical was creeping up for these two hearts. Sibila personifies a typical Portuguese lady. She is congenial, respectful and adorable. She is neither aloof nor rowdy nor does she use the F-word even when angry. Catch your breath for it is refreshing to find Rowan and Sibila chatting. It exhumes pure romance and leaves one thinking how warm these lovers are and that they must be twins. The rapport, fascination, charm, fairy tale mystery and joy that reveals itself makes one envious of the type of friendly atmosphere and laughter and jokes emanating from them. Sibila has beauty of heart and face one can hardly forget on meeting her. It was difficult for her, as well as for many people, to even believe that I was a qualified medical doctor because of the wretched look and demeanor life dolled me. It was not easy to phantom a doctor distributing adverts in the streets of Manchester and looking like a street person or a renegade vagrant/alcoholic needing food and descent clothing. Rowan did his best to get the story comprehensible to lovely sibila and friends.

I too came to like Sibila because of her good and friendly attitude, always smiling and ready to accommodate others. She always welcomes me with a broad smile that knocks the pain of day out and cheers me. She shows great respects for Rowan's friends and costumers and well all agree that Rowan was among few lucky men to land such an almost perfect partner to be with in life. These two are angels in human flesh I would keep as friends and I am eager to host them in the Gambia to serenade by my villagers. If Sibila was elated when Rowan proposed to marry her; I was in cloud ninety-nine for them. I was filled with joy that God had at last cemented their hearts for life. Meeting them left me with elation that they were made for each other and would be a perfect pair of lovebirds. They will definitely enjoy the relation for a long, long time to come. There is a special wedding present waiting for them when they visit me in the Gambia. The great day and wedding was announced in the following unique way characteristic of Rowan and Sibila. It in an open invitation to all Rowan said if you already know you are invited to Sibila's wedding and mine. We are getting married on Saturday the 12th of September 2009 in Sintra, just outside of Lisbon, Portugal and I want you to be there with us. Lisbon is a great place to go for a city break and if you want to the beaches any time Sibila and I will show you around.

The wedding took place as above and the couple is now happily resident in Lisbon, Portugal. Rowan Sheddon continued as a business tycoon in Lisbon while Sibila Sheddon, a lawyer, opened a huge law firm in the city of Lisbon and, in response to her catholic call, dose some missionary work in Africa.

Dr. Ceesay Displays first Book: The Legend

Against All Odds, published 2002

Dr. Alhasan Sisawo Ceesay, MD

Chapter 15

ALWAYS AND FOR EVER YOURS

Ramatulie Sey is a twenty three year old village development officer. Njawara village to her current post unanimously selected being uniquely a sympathetic and competent villager. Her suitor Ebou Gaye was a highly skilled weaver whose embroidery was unmatched by the competition.

They are both village birds for none ever visited Banjul, capital of the Gambia. They share extended families in Senegal and were together in Dakar on several times. Ramatulie found herself uneasy any time she was in the company of Ebou Gaye. Any time she set eyes on Ebou her heart plays frightening tricks in his presence. She initially tried to ward off the feeling but it became even more frightening when she ignores her sentimental weakness for Ebou Gaye.

She would draw or talk to attendance to distract her but her entire being was then more encouraged on paying attention to her would be future knight with shining Armour to sweep her feet to the bridal world. For a time both followed their trades with Ramutulie becoming frequent costumer of super weaver Ebou Gaye.

Ebou noticed some unusual relaxation in her part during one of her frequent shopping sprees. She relaxed her guard even though she knew that was foolish of her but she just could not help flirting for she loves the region's greatest and best weaver-man before her. Ebou Gaye being a shrewd fellow pretended as if he did not pick up her vibes and winks. He turned the tables by telling her a village development officer is always pleasant, as they smile and do their best and try everything they know even though they know very little. She retorted by letting him, "I know my job was needed by the community as it provide some guidance to the young, gives a helping hand to the elderly and prevent drugs over taking minds of the future generation. In addition without my field there would by now be streets flooded with pregnant teenagers and unwanted innocent babies left at street corners." Another customer witnessing the spark fueled it by encouraging her to enlighten the weaver. "Tell him he thinks he is the only specialized person in the entire region. This stern and candid response delighted Ebou for it tells him of her unselfish sincerity in her commitments. He already liked her but would keep it secrete until he learn more about her social life away from the job. It is obvious that she was pretty and one of the most popular if not revered girls in the village.

A lot of people are said to sort her opinion on matters important to their lives. Hence she would be a perfect partner and an asset to any who would be lucky to woo her. His turning the whole atmosphere away from her expectation made her nervous and believing that she had prematurely exposed herself to one that might not be interested in her. She asked, "Are you not guilty of punishing me for crime I was not guilty of." She added, "We cannot have civilization without mercy." These lines of thought threw Ebou into searching his mind on all that transpired and what made her state the above. This was female sagacity in full force as the intention was to keep her in his head and to force him request a rendezvous to clarify matters. Would it work? Well dear friend let us follow Ebou and Ramatulie' enamors trail. She bit her lip, started to feel exasperated with this tenacious weaver. She thought him blind to her moves and took a mile when given an inch of space. She blamed herself for having wishful dreams or thought about Ebou who might have his eyes and heart on another dame prettier than her. She thought it intelligent to learn to forget him and wait for her bright star to shine. The saying, "if wishes were horse beggars would gallop," almost applied in this case but love being blind and stubborn would not let Ramatulie give up as proposed.

Flooded with these vibes, inklings and exacerbated yearnings she decided to confide with the village sorcerer believing that an envier might have cast some sort of voodoo upon her. Normally these so-called people of the occult or spiritual communicators take great advantage of their clients who become their victims. Sure enough, upon contacting Witch doctor Kube Jarra, he pounced on the opportunity and concord with all fears and hypothesis put forth by Ramatulie Sey. He even added his own by letting her know that, "Jinamus, the most wicket of all devils, was assigned to make her disgrace herself by pursuing dreams of being bet rove to a male totally hostile to her request and equally disinterested in her." She was flabbergasted and begged Kube Jarra to do all within his power to ward off her torturers as well make them pay for their evilness. Oh! How sweet is revenge. The witch doctor took time to let her know that her detractors were years ahead of him and it would need hard work and lot of money to catch up and then undo the spell or curse cast on her. Kube Jarra was yet to tell either her disease or the treatment for it. He merely meandered around her mind to weave her into his tangled net. Once the victim is in it the execution and extortion goes on forever unless his victim is saved from his grip. Witch doctors epitomizes man's inhumanity to man.

They lie and cheat while, like vampires, shucking blood of their victims in broad daylight. On being certain that Ramatulie had swallowed both bate and hook, Kube Jarra told her, "You must first seek and bring the following rare pieces. They are:

1. A tooth of a Cyclopes serpent.

2. Tuff of a full grown lions' mare

3. A three-headed Cock

4. A none-striped baby hyena

This done the package was to be delivered at the crow of the Cock during dawn. The portion will be inactive the moment sunlight hits it." Yes, it was ridiculous request that kept victims coming over and over as Kube Jara normally give option to let him fetch the above for his clients at exuberant cost. They jump into the trap knowing they would not know where to start collecting the above outlined items in other for Kube Jarra to do his magic. The fee is multiplied by the difficulty entails in tracing the above. Kube Jarra tells his victims that his life was at risk but he would get it by hook or by crook in three months time. Once three quarters of D50, 000 (Dalasis) is advance immediately he disappears to Mali seeking the medicines.

Instead he buys another bride, cattle, and gold along with other house furniture before returning to continue his spotless lies and trickery. The victim is notified of his triumphant return and the need to bring along the rest of the fees when coming to commence treatment. In his absence, Ramatulie had serious discussion with her relatives and friends for them to chip in and help raise the balance due Kube Jarra. They all agreed that getting rid of Jinamus, the meanest devil of devil Dom was paramount in helping Ramatulie regain her sanity. Ramatulie was to bath daily for ninety days with concoction Kube handed to her. He guaranteed Jinamus running away from her forever. Who would not believe being told that hell will be removed and over in ninety days by means of bathing with concocted stench by the greatest sorcerer and renounced Witch doctor of the day. Hence, our lady did just as told hoping it would do the job of warding off her weakness for the weaver Ebou Gaye. To test if she has her freedom and success of the portion she deliberately paid an unexpected visit to Ebou's looms. He was no where to be found because he too had gone to consult his marabou Witch doctor as to why the lady he adores no longer come by his place nor has he seen her in the village for well more than ninety days.

Ebou' marabou only requested that he pull seven white kola nuts and give it as charity on a Friday to an old crippled lady in tattered rags. If done his bride to be will walk straight into his arms and remain his forever. Ebou paid D7000 and did as told. Three months later the two met at a cousins wedding. They each secretly tested their medicine's effect it had on the other.

Guess who cracked first? It certainly was Ramatulie whose love and weakness for Ebou intensified beyond earlier experience before her meeting the voodoo man. It was so intensive and overwhelming that she ran away to her uncle and confessed that her feelings were not that of a curse but true female's heart yearnings for the man she loves and wants to spend the rest of her earthly life with. She promised to refund their monies as soon as she get it but she no longer believed or agrees with Kube Jarra's lies and assertions.

This done; Ramatulie seek advice from a trusted old lady Mam Jarra, who was her late mother's confidant. Mam Jarra advised that she follow her gut feelings and true feminine instincts and do that which was best for her. In addition her friend Musu Tata also advised on similar lines and told her that she too had similar experience before marrying her current husband of twenty some years.

They have had their moments like happened in all marriages but he has always been there for her and the children. She loved him daily since setting eyes on him at the wrestling grounds. Both girls laughed leaving Ramatulie returning home very relieved and was found singing and laughing while at work the next day. This was seen as unusual for she had been very gloomy and moody in the past ten months. Ebou was slightly disappointed for Ramatulie failed to run into his arms as predicted by his grand Marabou.

He consoled himself in recalling the last bit the old marabou said; which was that the thing would take effect very slowly and that would be best as it would make the relationship last a life time. He too went home not too disappointed but hopeful that luck lurks round at time's corner. Three months would pass, with each of them becoming overly agitated for not seeing the other and not belling the cat. Soon the pussycat would be out of the bag for them.

The two finally came face to face at a cousin's wedding ceremony. First, Ebou asked, "Why did you stop coming to my work place? Was it something bad I said or wrong that I inadvertently did to you? You have deliberately stayed away from my loom.

I do have a special piece of embroidery or garment woven for you but could never find you for more than ten months."Dumfounded, Ramatulie, smiled and asked, "Can we discuss this at another pertinent time and in an appropriate place?" They then dispersed and sat among their peers but once on a while sending romantic glances and magical winks to each other that would melt the iron hearted and enliven the depressed one.

Ramatulie's friends noticed the magical weaver swinging from pole to pole and how Ramatulie would abruptly comment on the admirable features or movements made by Ebou. She was totally infatuated with him. As for Ebou, the slow ticking of the clock pressed him. He wanted this event to end so that he could talk to one he adores more than anything in this life.

He promised to do everything to muster all his male attributes and admit loving her. He only hoped that the melodrama to follow would not turn against him or be turned down by her. Even where that occurs, as most young women are normally shy of admitting their heart' wish when asked the first time, he would try and try as many times as it would take to let her accept him as her husband.The wedding ceremony of their cousin went on to the wee hours of the night canceling possibility of their meeting that day.

However, Ebou braved the turbulence and suggested that she drop by his loom noon the next day. Ramatulie concord and both went home with great windows of hope amid pounding impatient hearts. Ebou could not sleep that night as anxiety overwhelmed him. He kept wondering if she would accept a weaver as her husband knowing her prettiness, popularity and her standing in the village. Yet, why was he having such unquenchable feelings for her mounting upwards daily? Where they signals his marabou alluded to or should he return for more portions that would be potent and helpful in having him win his heart's darling? On the contrary Ramatulie slept like a baby. She woke up early, bathed and perfumed herself with one that has aroma only kings afford. The whiff of it lasted hours after she was well gone. People teased her and asked who was it that got into her heart for she smelled sweeter than a rose and looked prettier that day. She laughed and relished the observations while continuing her journey to the loom hoping that her dress and perfume would be equally additional weapons with which to nap Ebou Gaye out of his shocks for good. Indeed it worked for the first thing Ebou Gaye commented on upon their eyes meeting was how sweet she smells and jokingly asked if she would give him some of this perfume.

Well, well, if wishes were horses beggars would gallop. I think our lady friend was about to gallop to love lane and the bridal world. Before you know it they were embraced in each other's arms kissing, and kissing endlessly. Alas! Nature has spoken without a word being uttered from either party. In most countries far away from the source of the African continent and within many cultures such proximity and exuberant desire between lovers would have lead to instant uncontrollable exhilarating sex orgy. On the contrary in our village communities no sex until the day of the honeymoon is an unwritten law if not taboo every adult abide by. Failure to comply leads to undesired stigma and loss of respect from the society. Ebou Gaye did exactly as he promised on meeting Ramatulie. He looked straight into her eyes and told Ramatulie, "I have a confession to make to you along with the greatest request of his life." On hearing this preamble Ramatulie's heart went into over drive pounding well more than 300 beats per second. She was literally fibrillating. It almost choked her but she managed to hold her own to hear the rest of what was about to be delivered from the one she would do anything to win. His proposal was simple and to the point. In fact it was so short that it went by before she could digest and reflect its meaning or impact on her life.

She had hoped and waited for this moment all her adult life. She first took note and interest in Ebou Gaye when they were fourteen years old visiting extended families in Senegal some twenty years ago. He was never out of her romantic dreams and mindset since those tender teenage days. And today they stand hand in hand with him having proposed to marry her. It was heaven on earth for her and it took less than a split second for her to reply, "I gladly accept and would always and forever be yours till death". The two tangled and kissed over and over many times over before Ebou could extract himself, knowing that they were hence forth one, and told her, "I will ask my uncle and family scribe to buy kola nuts and formally meet your parents and uncles to request your hand in marriage and set the ball rolling for their wedding ceremony in five lunar months coinciding with end of the harvest."He jokingly added, "I do not want to be successful. All I ever wanted is Ramatulie, a nice house, a dozen kids and good dinners shrouded with love."It was too true to be real for her to fathom. She too lost no time in meeting with her family and shared the good news in secrete with them for this was high light of her life and dream come true for her. What a day! She and well-wishers sat down on the mat at her chamber and happily acknowledged the good news as they wriggled toes and laughed contentedly.

Some secretes never leave long as such once known by certain scribes. Soon rumors about the two being officially engaged ran wild in the community. Some secretly believed that she had fallen for a lower cast, as weavers were looked upon in those days, while others thought it outcome of blinding love and chemistry between the two lovebirds.

Some late comer ambitious males try to butt into the affair high handedly by offering her much more prestigious life and luxury her poor choused weaver would ever get in ten life times. She turned down all of them and asked them to stay away from being nuisances. She considers them as greedy, money-chasing, social-climbing scum bats she dislikes.

They developed an almost unholy respect for the power of money and concomitantly contempt of people without money. She had given her heart and soul to Ebou Gaye and would try to live her own life as just another human being. The village youths and middle aged along with her future husband respected her more for taking such courageous stand against intruding social fallacies, taboos and filthy rich of the district. A weaver was as good a husband as the king and a majority of community she leaved were more than delighted for her and choice taken.

This galvanized communities and an extensive preparation went ahead to kick start their forthcoming wedding, which would be a unique one for the entire region as it marks the braking of traditional barriers. The marriage was hastily arranged and the wedding took place five moons per schedule. The community sighed and was delighted that all went well for bride and groom who just had their honeymoon. Ramatulie, next day, sat besides her husband and dutifully kissed and gave a broad smile for she loves him very much. Ramatulie prepared herself to receive the promised reward from Ebou Gaye. That was what marriage was, being with your beloved and being at home anywhere in the world because you were with your lover. She added that not once would they ever be separated for a day. She repeated her love for him with a shy, happy glance and broad smiles. She authoritatively delivered the fine innate art of managing a husband. Their marriage lasted into their early eighties before Ebou Gaye left her for the next heavenly life in sleep. They had three boys and two girls all of who had by now their own families and grand children. Ramatulie still serve as matriarch of the family and they meet to celebrate life as bequeathed by their creator.

Chapter 16

THE MYSTRY BERE KOLONG QUEEN OF LOVE

At a region called Bere Kolong near Chakunda in the Badibous dwelled the most beautiful female figurine that only a few unfortunate young men chance to encounter. She is said to be parched amidst panorama of roses the like of which is found nowhere on earth.

Calamitous indeed for this sweetheart of the spirit chouses her lover and wards off any female that would dare flirt for her chosen mate. Her name was Jina Nyima, Alias Bere Kolong Masibo or the invisible spirit of love in the local vernacular. By the way Bere Kolong means stone well.

Jina Nyima was so tantalizing that any man other than the one she selected, gazing upon her is immediately turned into a stone at the position he stood. Hence up to today there stood many tall stones in the shape of men near bere Kolong.

Her method of recruiting a lover starts as early as when the male child was born. It is said that through her supernatural powers she would make her new male partner grow faster than most children, bigger, taller and normally a lot stronger than any of his peers.

She infuses these traits to send signal to other humanoid females who might set eyes on her lover. Jina Musa was Jina nyima's father and he regretted his daughter being in love with humanoids instead of Jini like her. Because of this irreconcilable state between them he cast a curse upon her and varnished to Jina Dou and never returns to Bere Kolong. Jina Nyima lived in a huge cave near the milky well whose waters served her. Only this milk like water quenches her thirst any other would leave her dehydrated and unable to function. It was reported that only one soothsayer or chief village Witchdoctor at a nearby village knew that the water from this particular source was her life being cursed by her father Jina Musa.

To secure her life she cast a guarding-spirit around the well making humans coming ten meters to it go blind instantly. Any who ventures beyond the ten-meter boundary are turned into stone, hence the name Bere Kolong in the local lingo. It sounded crewel that such a beauty would guard its jewel fiercely and so close to its heart. This no man's zone enables her to walk free and live free with the man of her heart. In this way, she literally steals her mate and keeps him kidnapped at the cave while feeding him the best kingly feasts and drinks from the heavenly milky waters of Bere Kolong.

In the event of any girl getting astray to the well to fetch water she is normally not turned into stone but her mind is cryptically controlled and she ends up being a servant at the cave. Should this servant chouse to have any feeling for her mate both are instantly blinded and turned into weeds to be fed upon by grazing animals. Jina Nyima is said to have many half-man and halftime mutants roaming about, especially at night. Villages claim to hear them singing and dancing or just playing magic to entertain themselves. The natives even believe that men with extreme physique amongst them may be her children she planted in the region. Friday the villagers for fear of angering the jubilant jinni kid accepted Friday nights as self-imposed curfew nights. The young jinni kids' playground was on top of mountain Kuku Konko near the famous Bao Blong creek. Atop of Kuku Konko balls of fireworks could be seen filling the night skies to the periled of any venturing to the sight. If any is seen one is normally surrounded by a powerful cyclone and swept to the cave to serve as slaves doing the chores for her mate. The mystery Jini dose not eats but needs the milky water to enable a human male to inseminate her. It serves as a sedative, which allows the process to take place. She is known to be the only Jini that copulates with human males.

I am told by an elderly lady that her secrete was unearthed by a young couple who for some odd reason were never affected by field of force that she surrounded herself while it petrified and blinded others. The elders believe it to be a challenge from her father. This couple choused such mundane place for romantic rendezvoused. They were so immersed in passion and love that jina Nyima was deliriously delighted watching them carry on, kiss, laugh, act frisky, mischievous, and at times crying over each other's shoulders. The jinni was amorous and affixed by the pantomime that unfolds before her from humanoids in love. In this of panoply of a paradoxical state paralleled to none the jinni queen is entertained. It represented a cavalcade of paroxysms in her life. In one hand she would instantly turn those who venture to cross the line at the periphery of Bere Kolong into stones for invading her territory. On the other hand this human couple was a source of joy and relief from normal jinni panoplies. It was a parody by which this pariah jinni takeoff her shoulders cumbersome load imposed upon her by jina Musa. To make certain of this entertainment, which by the way varies daily and always leaves her heart laden with love, envy, and a wish that she too was a human instead of the jinni race she belonged she rendered the couple immune to the spell around her sphere.

Some villagers reported that the Jinni queen and her human lover do at times change into human forms and adorned the most fancy dresses and join the villagers in their festivities, christenings, thanks giving, and even during burial rites. This jinni was one with human heart encased in a spirit that refuses to be with its kind. At the same time if any human makes the wrong move to wooing her mate she is delt with immediately. How do the innocent distinguish this icy hand of the stone hedges from real people? It so happens that one look at the couple reveals the tell tales of uniqueness not seen in any in the gathering. They look perfect in features, youthful despite notable advancing age, they still retain teenage voices, and they behave very maturely while saying very little at all. They are normally interested in the elderly and children but maintain short conversations with them. Hence this attribute leaves people suspicious and circumspect at all times when such figurines are in attendants. Above all, one or two well respected oracle or soothsayers would normally issue warnings to the likely hood that the couple may per chance appear at such gatherings well before the chosen date of the function. However, their presence was never the dooms day or as bleak as the oracles normally predicts.

At the middle or end of each function the jinni couple donates bags upon bags of money and clothing to the organizers and villagers leaving everyone happy and in welcoming spirit. The only missing part of the jigsaw is that there is that neither a village nor known address exists for this philanthropic couple. Amazingly al the villagers notice at the end of visit is sudden appearance of power cyclone marking their disappearance to batutodou before eventually returning to Bere Kolong.

In the end the villagers learnt to live with this phenomenon and those who bore baby boys leave the environment believing that might safe their from being kidnapped by the jini. They run to neighbours and relatives at villages hundreds of miles away until their child matures. I am told that this activity of kidnapping and breeding with ceased males continued for millenniums until one night when a ball of fire was seen to rise to the sky leaving behind it row after row of petrified and chard stones in human form or figurines surrounding Bere Kolong.

Some believe it to mark the death of the queen jinni daughter of Jina Musa. Up to today visitors to Bere Kolong could see stones, in similar fashion to the stone hedges, standing alongside the great Bere Kolong.

Some observers reported spotting one or two tears weeping while other figurines drone a smile at beholders. All in all and unto the present time no villager dares draw water from Bere Kolong for fear of angering the mutant jinni she left behind.

One good thing about the place is that modern day man had taken advantage and has turned the well into a tourist Mecca generating revenuer for the villages and the region. This then was the gift from the most bazaar romantic affair between jinni and man. The saying all is well that ends well hold true for this story the queen jini love.

Alasan Maballow Jr. with

Auntie Rohey Ceesay

Chapter 17

ROMANTIC SPELLS OF QUEEN ROSECALE

Fascination of the heart for another is a romantic realm deeper and mystical than can be imagined. Above all it assails infatuation and pushes our yearnings to greater heights. Best if the feeling is mutual and blossoms daily exponentially encompassing romantic spirit and God. On May first, in spring of 1990, two people, Alex and Rosecale, totally unknown to each other met in a National Express Coach heading for London. Neither expected to see a familiar face and had increased sense of loneliness to see so many unfamiliar faces in the bus. Normally sharing rows of seats in a bus connote no romance but for Rosecale and Alex it set the embers of love ablaze and burnt wildly since they set eyes on each other. The glow and emanating ecstasy following the meeting was nothing less than blessing from Aphrodite, the Goddess of love. The excitement, fantasy, sparkling smiles and hand holding all occurred in an atmosphere of deep, if not profound appreciation of the other. They grew from being total strangers to becoming the most envied and coveted relationship. First, let us peep at the commonality between these lovebirds. Both are highly educated and well into their middle years; had children and are devoted believers of their respective faiths.

Neither drinks alcohol nor smoke cigarettes but are lovers of music. They relish reaching out and helping others in need without being implosive. Alex and Rosecale are folks you want to befriend at the first encounter. They posses amiable social persona and attitude not only to themselves but also towards those they come across.

No wonder their hearts melted into each other at the first sight. Both knew then and therein that the feeling being experienced to be real and the moment should never be allowed to slip away. It was God's gift and chemistry that happened for them the moment they held hands in the coach on their way to London romantically glued to each other. An unspoken body language of love, yearning and friendship was all over their glances, motions, and smiles. Life was once again exciting and meaningful for both as their hearts merged silently. Soon the coach arrived at Victoria station in London and they exchanged contacts and vowed to keep in touch. Both agreed to meet in the soonest convenient time.

This spellbinding brief but magical encounter left them savoring raw love made in heaven. It was pure unadulterated love story Hollywood would love to film. Before long, series of calls went between these spirited lovers in cloud nine.

It would however not be until five days after their setting eyes on each other that Alex and Rosecale met for the second time, free of interruption and listening ears, and discussed their true feelings and yearnings openly for each other and mapped the way forward for the sustenance of their new found love. The meeting took place at the décor of the semi palace home of queen Rosecale. The quality of furniture, stereos and dining area speaks well for the taste of the occupier. The two had frank discussions on expectations and desire not to let this unique gift fade or walk away. They were free birds with the sky being the uncharted limits for them. They were rejuvenated by love and desire to please each other. If there was a heaven on earth, then this was it for them and they are not letting it go or ready to exchange it for any thing else. The brief meeting ended with both feeling happy and understanding that theirs was romance made in heaven. It was pure and blessed by the loving heart of God. Every minute was imbued as these lovebirds dedicated themselves to making it blossom more daily as long as they lived. On meeting Alex, I asked him how he felt about the whole experience and encounter and if he saw it viable. His response was a resounding endorsement and approval with total commitment to exquisitely beautiful queen Rosecale.

He adores her and sincerely believes she was a dream lady come true for him. He misses her a lot when she is away and feels happy, free and relaxed whenever he sees her or hears her melodious romantic soothing voice over the phone. He is convinced that queen Rosecale is the gem of his romantic experience in this life. With this 1000% commitment from Alex, I decided to arrange to interview spellbinding queen Rosecale before writing this story and chapter. Rosecale is ravishing, almost petrifying beautiful lady. She presents like a cross between an angel and one of the Greek Goddesses of love. She is amiable, simple and totally in love with Alex. Here is one of several responses to my simple question; Do you love your man and why? Rosecale unhesitatingly and unabashly replied, "I have given him my heart and soul eternally and I will do all in my power to be a good lover and friend in partnership during hard times and good times. Alex and I are henceforth one and a team for life". This was emphatic and convincing commitment matching that of Alex her male lover. Hence I will now let you reader sail the uncharted sea of love these lovebirds are at. Meeting these rare birds ushers a wealth of healthy cheers and happiness couched in abundant good spirit and atmosphere.

First, they decided to room together but Rosecale's place, being a common meeting ground for various organizations and patched with host of ladies activities, was not ideal. Hence, they opted to select the most suitable alternative rendezvous just for their pleasures and tranquility amidst the wing of love. Rosecale wanted no disturbance when with her lover. She wants to fully absorb and relish every moment they were together. This was her hour of enjoyment and letting loose into the pleasures of life. She felt being in cloud nine for having the rare fortune of getting an almost perfect lover. Alex, who could hardly bear being away from Rosecale, would equally not miss the adventure and he navigated deep into the recesses of her heart. Alex was a loving, sharing and equally good companion. There was a lot they shared and enjoyed each other's company. They only wished that they had met while teenagers or a lot sooner than this day. "Better late than never", said Rosecale. In the mornings, they take showers together with perfumed sprayed roses strewed all over the bath top. They sleep embraced all nights. They enjoy spoon-feeding each other at meals and even while at restaurants. Yes, these two daredevils of lovers are a unique romantic coincidence. They are never tired or bored of each other and every day together was a blessing cherished for life.

They have become intertwined twins linked heart to heart by the wild fires of love. Call them conjoined lovers if you may. Both wanted free time and free spirit for each other. They agree that among the best things of life is to have freedom to choose a lover. A bouquet of rainbow colored roses always welcomed Rosecale at the door on arrival to the love nest. Despite their advanced years they remain very young at heart and fully in love. The union of hearts went so well that Alex proposed marriage to Rosecale who found herself immersed in appreciation of the fact that things have grown to a better footing or more solid grounds that promotes and generates the relationship. To her the proposal cements them for good. They will never separate and to formalize the moment they prudently choused a civil wedding as the thriftiest under the current circumstances of the economic meltdown the world is experiencing. The great day came three months after Alex's proposal and went as planned. Only close family, friends, photographer and the presiding city Official attended. The ceremony and signing of documents took only twenty minutes and the couple walked out happy that they would be for each other for good. Friends gave them presents and there was brunch and buffet at the grand love hotel.

For the honeymoon Alex and Rosecale had decided to give them a treat they yearned but never could fulfill until their marriage. They decided to have a joyful whirlwind tour of the world. Yes, the trip took them right round the globe. It started from Paris, the city of romance, where they lodged at the hotel Amour in splendor for three days. They then visited the Touriefel and Palace du Verci along with many tourist sites in France. Next they flew to Delhi, India and visited the Taj-Mahal to enjoy the gift of love and wonders of the heart the then king had for his queen. The ornate marbles and golden tomb leaves one at awe and spellbind to remember for life. From India they proceeded to the golden domes in Moscow going as far as Siberia. The journey detoured to the great city of Beijing in China to allow them have a first hand encounter of Chinese culture and arts, and learn about its various dynasties. They both had desire to walk on the great wall and the trip gave them just that chance. Rosecale threw her shoes off and walked bare footed for ten miles on the great wall, which seems to stretch endlessly for thousands of miles covering vast areas of landscape, deserts and farmland. They relished the experience and on returning to Beijib and after a four days tour of the provinces Rosecale told Alex, "I will never forget this gift nor have such a thrill again."

Dr. Alhasan Sisawo Ceesay, MD

They now pushed onto Japan via Honking. They spent some time in Manela in the Philippines before flying directly to New York. The sleepless city of skyscraper commonly referred to as the apple city offered endless tourist adventures.

Among the places they visited were the United Nations buildings, the Rockefeller complex, Empire State building and many highly popular world shopping malls and centers. They attended theatres, and even danced at the Carnegie hall ballroom. From New York they landed in Washington D. C. the hub of political power in the USA and the world.

Here they went to the White House at Pennsylvania Avenue, home of the residing president, and took several pictures of the site and other attractions. In Washington the tour took them to the Congress, Library of Congress, Watergate, Howard University, George Town University and they went as far as Maryland some twenty odd miles away from Washington D. C.

After weeks of visiting popular sites in different American Cities the couples proceed to Canada via the Grand Canyon at the borders of the USA and Canada. They visited many Canadian cities and tourist region but the one that gave them a treat was journeying to Baffin Bay Island and living with the Eskimos for ten days.

They ate blubber and Walrus meat and slept in Igloos. Some thing they never dreamt that they are built and that their bodies could endure. It was another first in their lives for Rosecale always wondered how people like the Eskimos could survive the frigid tundra they came to call home. On returning to Anterior Canada, Rosecale tried her luck at a cooking completion at a Cuisine in Quebec. She came fifth but enjoyed herself and made lots of friends.

The trail now took the lovebirds to Australia and New Zealand. Here they found out that the saying "Down Under" was real for this part of the world was the last frontier before one drops to infinite space. They were landmasses far from any continent and have hundreds if not thousands of small Islands. Some of these Islands are still waiting to be mapped.

They enjoyed the Pacific and friendliness of the people of Australia and New Zealand. They spent few nights with the Australian blacks and found them very warm and eager to learn about other cultures. In New Zealand the couple went on fishing and surfing and joy boat rides. They left that region very pleased that they experienced the kindness of the people. It was like taking a trip to the bottom end of the world.

From the Pacific they flew to South America, visiting Argentina, Peru, Venezuela, Mexico, Uruguay, San Salvador and Panama Canal before boarding a luxury cruiser to Cuba and the West Indies Here they met face to face with effects of highhanded communism. Here only the party and the state mattered not freedom or democracy. It was a place and a world of constant belt tightening and vigilance that allows survival in this island nation.

The tour took Alex and Rosecale to sixteen Caribbean Islands spending more time in Jamaica, the Bahamas and Barbados before flying to Johannesburg in South Africa. In Africa natural beauty and panoramic nature of animals and humans unveiled itself to their pleasure. They were now in the real home of tribes and safari. For centuries Africa provided the fodder of dubious source of amazing tales from strange places across the seas.

The trip provided first hand clear and visible damage done to Africa and her tribes by unholy scrambles for colonies in the region. It left Africa fragmented and its public hungry and impoverished. The early writers portrayed Africa as land of Palms, Crocodiles and cannibals. The couple found this to be a sensational mythical twist of the truth about the beautiful black continent.

They did not find the villagers being wretched ingrates nor were they archaic as Tarzan movies depicted the villagers. The couple had the greatest spark and exciting moment of their lives when they met the Elder State-man of not only for South Africa but the world, President Nelson Mandela. He is today's bedrock of peace, compromise, tolerance, justice and democracy that brought Apartheid to its knees. Even though advanced in age and frail, he is still very charming and warm person indeed. Africa is proud of having sons like him. To no surprises the visiting couple took series of opportune photos with the madiva and had him autograph most of them for they know the photos will be worthwhile to have and to show friends back home in England. The next excitement came when the ANC tourist branch and propaganda wing of the ruling party invited them to state ballroom dance marking celebration of the newly ushered South African government. From South Africa they drove to Kenya, Sera Geti safari home of Africa, where they watched endless throngs of animals either gracing or just moving in their millions to other grasslands far away. This to them was nature's real zoo. The lines of these moving beasts stretch so far that they seem to merge with the blue skies of Africa. It is beauty of sight only seeing it life can one appreciates the panoramic splendor it yields.

They found and made new friends with villagers and school children in all places they visited, especially in Zulu land. From Kenya the couple proceeded to Lake Victoria and the Victoria Falls in Tanzania before heading for Nigeria, Ghana, Guinea Conakry, Mali, Gambia, Senegal, and Morocco, just to name few places they stopped on the way to the land of the Pyramids.

The final leg of this whirlwind world tour ended at the looming pyramids of Egypt. Yes, by this time the couple had seen, danced their hearts out with nearly every tribe and shook hands with tribal leaders, who is who in African politics and aspiring politicians on the way. It was a unique experience and journey.

It was educative if not exhilarating exposure to cultures. They relished the entire trip and even at times shed tears while biding goodbye to their friends as the metal bird took off from Cairo International for Heathrow. They were certain to miss all the friends and good life they found in these places.

Will they repeat the venture? You bet your bottom dollar they will if health and wealth allows it. At Manchester friends threw a surprise welcome mat and an all night party in cerebration of their tying the knot for good.

Njawara Banti Yassin

Chapter 18

AN ODE TO LOVE

Love, an instinct of adoration innate to man, is a unique phenomenon that almost sacrifices one heart to another. It is an adoration that touches the heart beyond any yearning. Love is the force that melts hearts into one and yet leaves the individuals intact. Love causes a mother who cannot swim to plunge head long into a raging river to safe her drowning child knowing she could drown with him. The embers of love keep us fired and restless about another. Love remains the most mystical relationship that can develop between two strangers. For the love of you I would give my heart as token of friendship one suitor told his future bride. Love is blind but the lover can never loose sight of the one that caught his or her fancy. Love and instinct is what cause ladies to go through pregnancy and risk of labour over and over till menopause. Love makes us affectionate, attractive and beautiful at heart. It is the most pleasant and devotional feeling one can have for another human being. It is a chemistry of the heart and mystery, which alchemists could not explain. Love is what makes the voice of one's lover sound like melodious music that none utters other than our lovers. Love has fueled our partnerships since recorded times. Love is our passions' slave.

Dr. Alhasan Sisawo Ceesay, MD

In biblical resonance Corinthian chapter 13, verses 4 – 8 it speaks of love thus: Love is patients. Love is kind. It dose not envy, it dose not boast, it is not proud, It is not rude and it is not self-seeking. Love is not easily angered and it keeps no record of wrongs. Love dose not delight in evil but rejoices with truth. It always protects, always trusts, always hopes and always preserves. Love never fails. William Shakespeare in Romeo and Juliet said of love as my bounty is as boundless as the sea. My love as deep, the more I give to thee the more I have, for both are infinite. Love is indeed the romantic spring that never dries for another, as it is greater than a feeling. It is a process that recognizes two hearts in continual desire for each other in laughter, trust, and sharing. Loving is sharing the world of life with another. It's a people unifier and is never empty or wasted as it opens the gates of happiness. There is no greater thing for two souls to feel they are joined to strengthen each other, to be one with each other in silent unspeakable memories of each other. I say love is the ultimate test of one's commitment to another. It is an unexplainable passion for another human. A solder commits his or her life for love of country and ideology like freedom and democracy. Love is the best gift we have for each other. Our kindness and love remains our legacy on earth. This reminds us that love is shared self-giving which end in self-remuneration.

Mother Teresa admonished us to spread love everywhere we go, to all children, families and next-door neighbours. Man falls in love partly to avoid solitude and withering away. It is said that love works wonders and in miracles as it weakens the strong and empowers the weak. A good example can be clearly adduced form story of the case of Dalila and Samson the giant.Love made the great brut Sampson to allow her cut a tuff of his hair, which rendered him instantly weak and lead to his eventual capture. A fit only love can deliver as armies tried but failed to conquer this monster of a man. Dose love Again, allow me serenade love by simply saying hurray to priceless love for letting me tick and feel for another heart in this life. All good things come to an end but true love lives forever. I love you with all my heart said a fiancé to her knight in amour. Hurray to priceless love.

not favour the weak one with passion in this case while at the same time destroying reason?

Love dose turn the world going in circles. Love goes with profound tenderness, which becomes at times almost insupportable. Love is self- sacrificing and responsibility between two. The more a partner gives the more rewarding the relationship becomes heavenly for them. Love is timeless and removes fear and encourages us to face challenges that would normally frighten others.

In short, dear reader, love for me is a free force, a spirit and part of a being needing to be fed by another's' heart to avoid it burning out. Love is neither a slave to king or servant; as it develops and dwells equally in both hearts and follows the laws of nature, which makes the sexes seek love.

It is hoped that this invigorating fairy tale of love left you ruminating on yours years gone by and that you enjoyed reading the work of a novice trying his hand at love story telling for the first time.

The tapestry of interwoven true love and fiction was generously bared to readers. The story makes us mellow and reminiscent our own days and love affairs. It is my hope that the above will let us allow the romantic flame, in us, alight day and night through life. Bless your hearts darling!

Chapter 19

Manding Medical Center

When God wants to destroy someone, He first made him an unusual dreamer. So Gandhi had his dream of people solving social deference none violently and Rev. Martin Luther king, jr. held onto his admirable dream of children of Jews and Gentile, black and whites holding hands and living in harmony spearheading peaceful cause for mankind. There are the Albert Schweitzer's and mother Theresa's of the world dreamers who spent their lives believing in their dreams for mankind. My dream, since 1956, was the simple goal of providing medical aid to those far and in remote villages. The villager, who is forced to walk miles on end to seek medical aid for his already dying child, wife or friend, deserves a better health system. Something I saw in 1956 left an indelible mark in my mind and I have since then asked and prayed that God help me bring part if not full to the kind of tragedy that was passing right before me. I was hopelessly unable to give relief except to comfort those involved. In 1956, while on my way to Saba village, I met an anxious father carrying his son and his almost dead pregnant wife on the back of donkey heading for the health center at Kerewan village, another three or more miles from where I met him.

The child was vomiting yellow stuff, he was sweaty, his eyes were reverted backwards and the pregnant lady groaning every time the mule moves. There was some greenish fluid dripping off her lapper. She could barely hold the ropes controlling the donkey. I went to Kerewan later that evening and asked about the status of that family, only to be told that the boy passed away half a mile to the dispensary and the lady was referred to the central hospital in Banjul but the family had no money to pay for her transportation nor was the River ambulance available as it was undergoing maintenance at the Dockyard. To cut a long story short, both child and mother died because of lack of medical facilities or modern medical aid to the villager. One or all of those lives could have been saved and remain beneficial to the country than the fate that befell them. I prayed and grieved with the family for months and redoubled my efforts at school in other to solve such development in future. I committed myself to medicine from that day on and never regretted making such a challenging decision in my life. Hence, when on the day I was taking the Hippocratic Oath, I not only swore to uphold all therein but to make sure that God help me not to ever deviate from my commitment and promise to be part of the solution in the health services of the Gambia, to foster health education for the villager, and to complement the existing medical facilities in the Gambia as well as ease the shortage of medical service personnel. To many, except the dreamer, such Erewhons leads to failure as they turn to be white elephants. Some friends tease me by flatly promising to rise from their graves on the opening day of such an Alice in wonderland project. Let me make it crystal clear that I had no elusions about what was needed, or to be done and that the building of the hospital would indeed be a lifetime challenge I am fully ready to grapple with. There would be a lot of well-wishers but very few will ever want to join until the opening day ceremonies. So first things first, I met an attorney friend Mr. Ousainou Darboe, a villager like me, on September 24, 1992, and pleaded for his assistance with the legal aspects of setting up a charitable foundation, Manding Medical center at Njawara village in the provinces for the sole purpose of providing much needed medical aid to the villager. He was very obliging and requested no payment in return for his services. In the mean time I got a board of governors elected while he prepared the memorandum and articles of association of Manding Medical Centre at Njawara village. Also, I met with the Lower Badibou district chief, Kitabou Singateh, who by the way was my primary school class mate at Kinte Kunda from 1953 to 1957, the District Authority, Commissioner and the kerewan Area Council.

Dr. Alhasan Sisawo Ceesay, MD

All of whom were more than delighted and did all they could under the law to help me set up a grassroots local advisory committee, which was headed by the commissioner, to assist the board and also let the villagers feel being part of the ongoing project. At my home village, Njawara, a group organized itself and formed a pioneering committee to formally ask the Alkalo (village head/mayor) and the people of Toro Bahen village to donate the earmarked land between it and Njawara for the sole purpose of establishing the Manding Medical Centre on it. The land issue was partially cleared by the first week of the appeal. In October 1992, Alkalo Omar Koi Bah of Toro Bahen, along with alhaj Musa (Njabi) Bah and Sirimang Bah called my brother, Doudu Ceesay, the elders of Toro Bahen and I to officially inform us that the earmarked land of two plots have been donated to me for the sole purpose of erecting a medical center and hospital facility for the villagers of the region and Gambia. We thanked him for his foresight and kindness towards future generations. I went back to my lawyer, Ousainu Darboe who by then had finished all work needed for the registration of Manding Medical Centre. We are forever indebted to Alkalos Omar Koi, Arfang Bah, Musa (Njambi) Bah and resident Sirimang Bah, and the people of Toro village.

Lastly but not the least our venerable able lawyer Mr. Ousainou Darboe, without whose kindness and legal mind the registration of Manding Medical Centre would have taken longer that it did assisted me. I also express profound gratitude to the Hon. Chief of Lower Badibou district, Kitabou Singateh, the commissioner, and the local district authority for their understanding and willingness to contribute positively towards our goal and growth.

I submitted the registration application material to the Attorney General's Chambers at the Justice Department, Banjul, on October 22, 1992 and Manding Medical Centre was officially registered as an incorporated charitable organization under the companies Act, 1959 by the 27th of October 1992. Manding Medical Centre' certificate of incorporation is number: 224/1992. With the completion of the paper work and registration of the center, I embarked on a blitz of letter writing informing philanthropists and organizations worldwide about Manding Medical Centre and the need for assistance or donations of medications, equipments, medical videos with which to teach our cadre and villagers to become health worker or evangelist, or nurses and to help us build the center.

To complete the establishment process, after the land was officially ours, I wrote to the following letter to the Ministry of Health informing them of the formation of Manding Medical Centre, a self –help health organization at Njawara, Lower Badibou, North Bank Division, the Gambia. Our temporal address was at 5B Ingram Street in Banjul, capital of the Gambia.

Manding Medical Centre

5B Ingram Street

Banjul, The Gambia

March 2, 1993

Permanent Secretary

Ministry of Health

The Quadrangle

Banjul, The Gambia

West Africa

Dear Permanent Secretary,

Re: Application for the establishment of a Medical Centre at Njawara in the North Bank.

Njawara Banti Yassin

We are pleased to bring to attention the setting up of a self-help Health organization in the North Bank Division at Njawara village. The directorates and members of the organization would be more than grateful if the Ministry of Health would allow us establish Manding Medical Centre at Njawara village, Lower Badibou District of the Gambia.

Manding Medical Centre, when fully operational, will provide medical, surgical, gynecological and obstetrics, Pediatrics and other facilities to the villagers. It will also help ease the shortage of medical facilities in that region. Manding Medical Centre will have health education secessions in the villages as an effort to enlighten our youths.

Again, thank you for taking time to consider our application and we certainly look forward to a positive recognition of the need for such a center in the rural sector of the Gambia.

I am anxiously waiting to hear from your office at your convenience. Regards

Yours sincerely

Dr. Alhasan S. Ceesay, MD

Director/Coordinator

Meanwhile the villagers grew more enthused and throngs of them attended our monthly health field trips or clinics. The attendance grew so large that we ended up listing the villages to attend in turn of nine villages per trip. This usually totals to a bit above 1,000 patients at a given visit.

I normally go on weekends with three doctors and at times four volunteer doctors along with Nurses aid Mrs. Mbee Sonko and Ida Njie to assist us do the job. The field trips/clinics start with an announcement by Radio Gambia giving the names of villages expected to attend and at which village health center.

The clinic day starts with an early morning breakfast by the team and then a ride to the village health center where we would find the villagers and their sick ones assembled. Every occasion starts with the offering of prayers and then the various village heads, in attendance help us in organizing the flow of people wanting to be see by one of our team doctors.

In most cases the day goes trouble free but at certain localities the political tension does make it very difficult to have such large groups of people without little arguments. Thanks to the Commissioner (s) for deploying the police or making them available to quell trouble and help us maintain order during these clinics.

Njawara Banti Yassin

Commissioner Lamin Koma can tell you how rough things can be at some of these clinic centers. He was trapped in one of these bad moments of people rushing to be in the front line of the queue to see one our doctors. The Ministry of Health finally sent us the following affirmative reply as thus: -

Ministry of Health & Social services

The Quadrangle

Banjul, The Gambia

Ref.P510/289/01(95)

Dr. Alhasan Ceesay

Manding Medical Centre

5B Ingram Street

Banjul, The Gambia

RE: Application to establish a Medical Centre at Njawara

I acknowledge receipt of your letter of the 2nd March 1993 on the above-mentioned subject. I wish to inform you that this Ministry has no objection to your application to establish Manding Medical Centre at Njawara.

This initiative is in line with our national health policies and we would render our support in our joint efforts to improve the health of the people.

Signed: N. Ceesay

For Permanent Secretary

After several more field trips it was suggested we apply for a None Governmental Organization (NGO) status. It was believed that if we become and NGO, help would come our way quicker.

I went to work on this suggestion and arranged for Tango Secretariat Centre to send one of the United Nations voluntary program officers to come and evaluate our performance relative to the objectives of Manding Medical Centre. This was accepted and a field trip was set up for September 12 to 22, 1995.

Radio Gambia made the announcement well ahead of the time for our arrival and the following was the outcome of that august gathering of September 21 &22, 1995.

Chapter 20

TANGO SECRETARIAT TRIP REPORT ON MANDING MEDICAL
CENTRE, SEPTEMBER 21 – 22, 1995

A field trip to Kerewan at the North Bank Division was organized by the Manding Medical Centre Executive Director Dr. Alhasan S. Ceesay in conjunction with Tango Secretariat Centre to see the organization's activities and meet the members before recommending the organization as a member of Tango.

On September 21, 1995, two meetings were organized in two big centers where members gather to air their views and experience from the organization. Alkalos, chiefs, imams, women, men and youths attended these meetings. The key leadership from five villages in their speeches showed interest and support for the project and organization.

Alkalo of Toro Bahen Omar Koi and chiefs donated the land for the constructing of Manding Medical Centre, the hospital and its ancillaries. The two meeting were highly attended and successful.

The Tango (UNV) program officer Mr. Muloshi on behalf of Tango gave a keynote speech on Tango's operations and activities as an umbrella organization and urged members to work hand in hand with the organization in their efforts to develop their villages and North Bank area.

The three meetings with the commissioner during the field trip on our courtesy call were successful and encouraged the executive Director of Manding Medical Centre, Dr. Alhasan Ceesay, to cooperate with the strict, especially the commissioner who is one of the advisors in the local committee.

The commissioner thanked Tango for making the purpose of the mission clear to him and promised that he will try by all means to cooperate with Tango in the area of Technical advice and institution capacity building. Clinic day was organized on September 22, 1995 at Njawara and 150 people attended and got treatments.

RECOMMENDATION

Looking at the caliber of leadership and development activities compared to some NGO tango members in comparison to Manding Medical Centre, the organization need consideration since they have already activities with a promising future.

Looking at the composition of the Board, they have people with a great vision. They have strong membership and backup at the grassroots levels. The organization has chosen to do what is right at the right time and their concentration in one area is vital and a good starting point. Any success achieved by any organization depended on good leadership and discipline. Manding Medical Centre has quality leadership and deserves NGO status.

Signed: M. Muloshi

UNV Program Officer

We were delighted by the recommendation made by the United Nations voluntary Program Officer in the Gambia. We redoubled our efforts to contact organizations seeking help worldwide. In between letters and monthly field trips to different select health centers we were blessed with visits from interested friends and groups or representatives of similar organizations in the globe. I had several telephone calls to Dr. Edward Brown, an official of the World Bank in Washington, D. C. responsible of the bank's health affairs at the time.

He was very receptive and had several added discussions with Dentist Melvin George, then Director of Medical and Health Service for the Gambia, on how the bank could help in the financing of the building of Manding Medical Centre.

These talks went on well and Dr. Edward brown gave me his promise and personal commitment to helping the project and that we have to start in a small scale and the building will have to be done in several well planned phases. Dr. Sidi C. Jammeh, a former Armitage School colleague, promised to help me by constantly reminding Dr. Brown of the need to help us with the project.

This kept the momentum at the World Bank alive for Manding Medical Centre. Among our guest were a couple from Colchester, Essex, UK, Lorna V. Robinson and husband Keith Robinson were very impressed by our project and enthusiasm of the ordinary villagers about Manding Medical Centre.

They fell in love with the idea and objectives of the self-help health organization and promised to help as much as they could. We had by this time submitted application for NGO status and ACCNO Secretary replied thus:

Njawara Banti Yassin

ACCNO Secretariat

Dept. of Community Development

13 Mariner Parade

Babjul, The Gambia

September 12, 1994

Ref.CD/ACCNO/Vol3/(183)

Dr. Alhasan S. Ceesay

Director/Coordinator

Manding Medical Centre

P. O. Box 640

Banjul, The Gambia

Dear Sir,

RE: application for an NGO status within the ACCNO framework

Dr. Alhasan Sisawo Ceesay, MD

Please find enclosed a self-explanatory letter from the Ministry for local government and lands concerning the approval of your application for NGO status. ACCCNO Secretariat congratulates your organization for successfully completing the registration process and wishes you a fruitful relationship in the field of development.

Thank you for your cooperation

Yours Faithfully

Musu Ngujo

For: ACCNO desk Officer

Cc: file & R/File

Replies from our worldwide appeal letters did not pour in money nor did they materialized beyond promises to help in due course. Hence, I decided to open up a pharmacy at my expense at my residence in the Bundung area of Serekunda using the proceeds from its sales to finance the health field trips and activities of the organization. This meant spending an extra three to fours at the pharmacy daily after eight hours at the RVH before rejoining my family.

All drugs used for the treatment of patients at our field trip clinics were purchased from sales I made at the Bundung Pharmacy. A local agency, known as IBAS, lent me D8000, interest free, which was used in buying drugs and paying for transportation for the project's activities. The loan was completely repaid well ahead of the allowed sixteen months period given by IBAS.

We are obliged and grateful to Aja Ndey Oley Jobe and management of IBAS for their kindness to assist us at the time. Just when things were about to be financially complete for us to start the first phase of building the various sections of the hospital, came the unexpected coup d'etat of July 22, 1994. The reaction from would be our donors and supporters or sponsors were swift and equally unexpected.

All those who were considering giving the project a chance sited likelihood of sudden national unrest and instability as reasons for their withdrawal of promised aid and participation while some suggested my waiting until after the transition phase of the coup d'etat before they would reconsider reopening our files with them.

Again it resorted to legend or case of the chicken the egg, which came first as no one, knew when the transition would end and we kept our fingers crossed hoping that daylight will be ours in not far distance. It was a severe blow to our hope and for getting the type of interest and support that was engendered for Manding Medical Centre would be difficult to match after such crisis that occurred in the Gambia.

Many were acting in conjunction with their governments, which were not sure of what the future under military rule would be for the Gambia. All prospective and possible international sources earmarked for Manding Medical Centre were either frozen or evaporated into thin air with the coup leaving me floating in the middle of the ocean of despair without a life jacket except God's merciful hands.

I knew the villagers would grow restless if nothing happens in the direction of building the center. I called an emergency general meeting with members from most of the villages and told them of the new challenge and development and this information not only fell on deaf ears but left their spirits dampened.

Interest waxed and waned at some quarters but I kept on trying my best not to be despondent like the others have shown. I kept the organization alive under very limited funds raised from the pharmacy at Bundung until my trip to the UK in January 2000.

Before leaving the Gambia, the Commissioner for north Bank Division and chairman of the local advisory committee for Manding Medical Centre, Mr. Lamin Koma, gave me the following letter to assist me in my fund raising drive while in England and possible other European countries. It read thus:

The Commissioner

Kerewan Village

North Bank Division

The Gambia, West Africa

June 15, 1998

TO WHOM IT MAY CONCERN

I hereby write to testify and confirm that Manding Medical Centre is a self-help health project situated at Njawara village, North Bank Division.

Dr. Alhasan Sisawo Ceesay, MD

As the Commissioner of this division I was elected as the Chairman of the local advisory Committee of the Manding Medical Centre. As I am concerned, I am aware of this self-help project since it took off the ground, by the able hands of Dr. Alhasan S. Ceesay, a born citizen of Njawara village.

The purpose of the establishing of such a medical centre is to provide medical attention/care to all Gambians irrespective of religion, tribe, nationality or gender and age within the country and sub-region.

It is in these regards that this office writes to seek for your assistance in providing support in cash/kind to make this medical center a reality. I look forward to your continued support and cooperation.

Signed: V. Baldeh

For Commissioner

North Bank Division

The new millennium started with good omen for Manding Medical Centre. I have been invited to go to Europe and America on a found raising trip for the center but could not because of my commitment with the Royal Victoria Hospital (RVH).

I needed a longer action period to be able to travel and keep my job at the sane time. Above all my family needed the monetary support, which would fade away if I lost the post at the RVH. Hence, to my delight and greatest timely occurrence I heard from my long-standing friend in Colchester, Mrs. Lorna V. Robinson, inviting my wife and I to come to the UK to attend the wedding of their younger daughter on January 9th, 2000. Coincidentally, I had just started my annual leave, which was to finish on the 26th of January 2000.

The excitement mounted when we received a fax from the visa officer at the British High Commission in the Gambia requesting that we report to the visa processing office with our passports on Tuesday 8.30 am January 4th, 2000 for processing of our visas for our pending travels to the UK.

This took me by surprise because of the casual way we had discussed the possibility of such a trip. So when we got the telephone call followed by the said fax from the visa section I was caught off guard and had to rush through all the preparations for my wife and I to travel to UK without a second thought on whether adequate arrangements were being made for my eventual pursuit of a postgraduate degree (MRCP) in internal medicine.

Hind side has it that I needed to discuss this aspect with the visa councilor and request for eventual student visa status or leave to remain until my completion of the post graduate degree I wanted to pursue.

Miss Famatanding Ceesay, Daughter

God's ways and timing are best for every occasion. I was yearning to get a way out of the financial limbo the center ran into since the change of government in the Gambia. Now that opportunity was suddenly thrown on my laps by Lorna Robinson's open-ended invitation for my wife and to attend their daughter's wedding ceremony in the UK.

Interested donors started being weary about Military rule and possible restlessness that may ensue. Hence, Manding Medical Centre literally lost all its prospective overseas support as well as sponsors most of who had cold feet after the July coup d'etat of 2004.

I ended up running the center from my meager salary of D1500 or seventy-five pounds sterling per month and of literally hard labor with long hours at a time. The other source was from what little I could make from sales at the Bundung pharmacy.

To cut a long story short we were granted visas to travel to the UK. We left the Gambia on the 6th of January 2000 on a new footing and challenge to bring back some life into Manding Medical center while in England. I got on the ball as soon as the wedding ceremony was over. I obtained a three–year study leave from the Management Board of the Royal Victoria Hospital in Banjul.

This gave me all the time I needed to try to rekindle interest in the center and thereby inject into Manding Medical center cash flow it needed to help us meet or our targeted goal and objective for the farming community in the North Bank Division of the Gambia. It was more like a miracle entering this new concrete and direct ways. Help from my host Lorna Robinson of Colchester, Essex, UK further anointed my hands.

Lorna and I wrote several letters to various places, including celebrities and organizations, most of who replied in the negative because of perception they had about the political climate in Gambia since the coup d'etat of July 22nd 1994.

Nonetheless some hinted being interested at a later date, meaning when the solders return to camp. A few donated small amounts plus hospital items. By now it became clear that we have to counter the perception most, on this side of the isles feel or had about the Gambia at the time.

This dreadful start did not alarm me much for I am fully aware of the wrong information about the average African in the village, who like most, is just a descent human being trying to earn an honest living for himself, family and community.

Villagers are least interested in all the political gimmickry shrouding and clothing their lives. I do not at all blame the rest of world for getting sick and tired of helping and not seeing any tangible good come out of it and worse some African politicians and regimes show no interest in helping move the African people onto better and modern rewarding modalities of life.

They offer more lip service than opening avenues for progress. How many knew that the Ethiopian starvation was politically orchestrated by the then Mangestu regime? Genocide regime and the heartlessness of some African politicians made me feel sick.

To remove any possible skeptics regarding Manding Medical Centre and its objectives we decided to have it registered as a charitable organization in the UK under the name of Colchester Friends of Manding charitable trust. The Robinson knew a solicitor who would be so kind to help us with the legal aspect of the registration process with UK charity Commission.

They spoke to Mr. Bruce Ballard of the Birkett long Solicitors to come to our aid. This kind gentleman, like my lawyer friend, Mr. Ousainou Darboe, gladly agreed to help and sent us a draft of the Trust deed.

After a series of changes were made on the draft he forwarded our request to be registered in the UK as a charitable organization helping its twin partner or parent group, Manding Medical Centre at Njawara village in the Gambia, West Africa. Meanwhile, we concentrated our activities through media campaign effort to call attention to existence of Friends of Manding and their desire in building a hospital for Manding Medical Centre at Njawara, the Gambia. Again we ran into a very gentle heart in the person of Miss Helen Anderson of Colchester who was the Community website editor for Essex County.

She went head over heels regarding the idea of helping others so far away when approached by Lorna Robinson. Helen thought the idea wonderful and at the same time helped us have our own website and also had an article published by the Evening Gazette which had a large reader circulation. In the same vein I got the interest of Dr. Linda Mahon-Daly, Dr. Peter Wilson, Dr. Laurel Spooner, Dr. Richard Spooner, Dr. Philip Murray, Dr. Barbara Murray, Dr. Fredric Payne, who by the way was our Medical superintendent under who I worked at the RVH during the later part of colonial Gambia, along with many surgeries in the Colchester area.

These were my Good Samaritans of the day who worked acidulously to make Manding Medical Centre become a reality for the villagers in the Gambia. Dr. Linda Mahon-Daly helped distribute letters about Manding Medical Centre to nearly all her colleagues in the Colchester Borough and so did Dr. Laurel Spooner. Bless their hearts for kindness and job well done.

The news article published by the Evening Gazette brought us another very helpful and kind person, Mr. Malkait singh who is an ophthalmologist and had made several trips to the Gambia before knowing about the Friends of Manding. He was delighted to join Neville Thompson, Connie Thompson, Lorna Robinson, Keith Robinson, Loenard Thompson, Mark Naylor, Barbara Philips and others as pioneering members of Friends of Manding.

Mr. Malkait Singh and I grew to be very good friends and he had since given me lots of personal monetary help to cater for my exams and family back in the Gambia. I am very grateful for interest and kindness, and concern he showed about my family.

A few months after the formation of Friends of Manding, Dr. Laurel Spooner spent a week in the Gambia vacationing and doing some fact finding about the center.

During which time she visited Manding Medical Centre at Njawara in the North Bank Division. The villagers were happy to meet her and thanked her about good work being done in Colchester regarding Manding Medical Centre.

Everyone was happy about the news that people in the UK were poised to assist Manding Medical Centre goes forward in its drive to provide medical aid to villagers. A meeting of member of the Friends of Manding was scheduled for the first week of February 2001.

 Mean while our solicitor continued pressing for registration of Friends of Manding, which is the arm and Manding Medical Centre's Colchester branch support group, as charity in the UK.

Dr. Laurel Spooner suggested we start with small-scale form of the center and then gradually expand as funds become available. This consideration would be studied in full and deliberated upon by the committee during the forth-coming February meeting.

Keith, Dr. Ceesay, and Mrs. Lorna Robinson

Miss Binta Ceesay, Daughter

Chapter 21

WHAT IS MANDING MEDICAL CENTRE?

Manding Medical Centre, located at Njawara village in the North Bank Region, Gambia, West Africa, is a self-help village health organization founded by Dr. Alhasan S. Ceesay. Its objective is to provide medical service to the villagers by providing efficient and affordable medical aid to all people in and around the Gambia, especially the rural sector.

We are dedicated to relieving suffering and ensure effective treatment for villagers and all attending Manding Medical Centre at Njawara, NBR.

ESTABLISHED

The Manding Medical Centre is founded by Dr. Alhasan Sisawo Ceesay, a native of Njawara village in 1992, because of sheer shortage of medical service to the region and the preponderance of premature deaths by children from Malaria, malnutrition, diarrhea, and worm infestations. These childhood maladies account for almost 25% of Gambian children's death before the age of five years.

Dr. Alhasan Sisawo Ceesay, MD

The Gambia Ministry of Health officially recognized the Centre in 1995 and prior to which it became a None Governmental Organization (NGO) on September 12th, 1994. In addition, the Manding Medical Centre now has Friends of Manding Charitable Trust, Colchester, Essex, UK as its arm and liaison in the UK and the European Union countries. The Friends of Manding is a registered charity in England and Wales. Its registration number is 1088136 since August 21, 2001.

In similar development and purpose, Dr. Avery Aten heads the Friends of Manding Alpena Charitable Trust, Alpena, Michigan, UAS since May 2005.

MISSION STATEMENT

Suffering in another human being is a call to the rest of us to stand in fellowship. It requires us to be there and it is a mystery, which demands the spirit of caring, sharing and our presence. Our duty as healthcare professionals is providing medical care, which is a fundamental right of all human beings. This village health organization is dedicated to providing medical aid to the rural sector and farming community in the Gambia. It will compliment the health service in the Gambia in addition it will promote preventive medicine in the hinterland of the Gambia.

Njawara Banti Yassin

MEMBERSHIP

Well over twenty thousand villagers, comprising of farmers, village heads, and chiefs, the Kerewan Area Council, Commissioners and local District Authority are now fully active enthusiastic members of Manding Medical Centre.

All are welcomed to join the endeavors of the center. People from the rest of the globe are more than welcomed to participate or share with us our dream in bring much needed medical service to people in desperate state because of lack of medical facilities.

ACTIVITIES

Manding Medical Centre tries to alleviate some of the above mentioned health problems and situations by having bimonthly health field trips/clinics to villages teaching them about health, preventive medicine and hygiene that would help reduce the number infected and the vectors responsible for these diseases.

We encourage antenatal and postnatal attendance of clinics by mothers and we treat the sick amongst them with minimum charge to not so elderly and pregnant young ladies.

The service is free to children, the very elderly, and the indigent needing emergency treatment. The rest pay amounts well below tat in private practice. Money accrued is subsequently used to buy drugs with which to treat the patients and for other projects of the center. When in cession the center treats well more than 1000 patients per field trip to the villages.

We provide free information and advisory service on aids and sexually transmitted diseases (STDs) to the young, all patients, their relatives and friends. We also plan to have a Nursing School in due course to augment not only staff but also the government health centers when the need arises.

IMMEDIATE GOAL AND APPEAL

The villagers are very enthused about the center and Toro Bahen village, next to Njawara village, has donated two plots of land for the building of the center and its ancillary units, which is now leased to manding medical center for ninety-nine years. More than 2000 children die tragically from malaria and other childhood ailments stated above for shortage of health services.

Njawara Banti Yassin

We are eager to start building the children' and maternity wings of the proposed Gambia General Hospital at Manding Medical Centre and do need raise the required 900,000 pounds sterling to accomplish our goal. Ten bags of cement cost thirty pounds sterling or $60 (sixty us dollars). Also we would be most grateful if we could be assisted with medicines and equipment to facilitate our work. Hence we implore you to kindly support our yearning to build the children' and maternity wings of Manding Medical Centre.

We are dedicated to providing medical aid to the villager, especially children. We are investors in people and you are invited to join the endeavors of Manding Medical Centre at Njawara village, the Gambia, West Africa. Help us make a difference and beacon of hope for the villagers. Please give generously. Today's hope can be tomorrow's reality. We want to contribute positively towards the health services of the Gambia, and with this center in place it will create greater health awareness and privation by the villagers. Cash contributions of any amount should be sent in the name of Manding Medical Centre, to the Friends of Manding charitable Trust, 82 Finchingfield Way, Blackheath, Colchester, Essex, CO2 OAU, and England.

Dr. Alhasan Sisawo Ceesay, MD

It is vital to be certain that Dr. Alhasan S. Ceesay is informed of your contribution via email thus: alhasanceesay@hotmail.co.uk. Your kindness and humane consideration to help save lives will always be deeply appreciated and grateful for by the villagers, the Gambia and I.

OVERSEASES LINKS

The Friends of Manding in Colchester, Essex County, UK, is formed by a local group of residents, doctors, and nurses who regularly visited the Gambia and is in support of Manding Medical Centre. Manding medical center through the auspices of the Friends of Manding recently received recognition and registration by the UK Charity Commission.

They serve as support and our liaison in the Europe Union. The Friends of Manding in behalf of Manding Medical Centre at Njawara has been entered in the central Register of charities with effect from August 21, 2001; the registration number is 1088136 for England and Wales.

Also, a similar charitable trust, the Alpena Friends of Manding Charitable Trust of Michigan, USA, has been established in Alpena, Michigan in June 2006.

It's headed by Dr. Avery Aten a resident physician chairman of the Women and newborn of the Alpena region Community Health along with the medical community of Alpena.

Ntoro Bahen village, Badibou, NBR, The Gambia

Chapter 22

MANDING MEDICAL CENTRE MILESTONES

Manding Medical Centre has been in my mind's drawing board since the early 1950s but it took off in earnest when I returned to the Gambia, after graduating from medical school in 1992. The Centre is registered as a charity with the Attorney general's Office, Department of Justice, Banjul, The Gambia, since 1993. The Gambia Ministry of Health also recognized it in the same year. Toro Bahen village, Lower Badibou, NBD, Gambia, donated two huge plots of land for the location of the center in 1993. Our nongovernmental (NGO) status was approved in 1994. On September 21, 1995 Tango Secretariat sent a United Nations voluntary program Officer, Mr. Muloshi on field trip to evaluate the organizational and extent of support for Manding Medical Centre at Njawara village. Mr. Muloshi's recommendation after two days field trip to the region stated thus; "Looking at the caliber of leadership and development activities to some NGO Tango members in comparison to Manding Medical Centre, the organization need consideration since they have already activities with a promising future. Looking at composition of the Board, they have people with a vision.

They have strong membership and backup at grass root levels. The organization has chosen to what is right at the right time and their concentration in one area is vital and good starting point. Any success achieved by any group or organization depends on good leadership and discipline. Manding Medical Centre has high quality leadership and deserves NGO status".

It was not until my travels to the UK in 2000 that the Friends of Manding Charitable Trust was formed and registered as charity in England and Wales by the UK Charity Commission. Friends of Manding is the extended arm of Manding Medical Centre at Njawara, The Gambia. They serve as our liaison in the UK and the European Union. Please browse on our website thus: http://friendsofmandinggambimed.btck.co.uk, to learn more or for further information about our work and organization.

We are still on fund raising activities to earn enough to enable us build the children' and maternity units of the hospital at Manding Medical Centre at Njawara. In May 2005, 11 American students and their instructor Mr. Thomas Ray visited Manding Medical Centre at Njawara.

Additionally, input from has now resulted in Alpena City, Michigan, USA, twining by proclamation with Njawara and Kinte kunda villages in Gambia respectively on the 5th of December 2005.

In June 2006, Dr. Avery Aten, Chairman of the Women and Newborn of Alpena Region Health Community along with the medical community of Alpena commenced processing application for a charitable Trust to be named Alpena friends of Manding Charitable Trust, Michigan, USA.

This will soon be finalized and up and running to help Dr. Alhasan Ceesay in the provision of medicine and educational assistance to schools in the Lower Badibou district, the Gambia, West Africa.

In August 2008, Dr. Alhasan Ceesay and the Badibou Cultural Dance Troupe will visit Alpena and other cities in Michigan for fund raising drive to enable the building of the Manding Medical Centre children and maternity units at Njawara village.

Dr. Richard Bates, an Obyng, and a number of medical professionals involved in obstetrics and gynecology at Alpena, Michigan joined Manding Medical Centre's crusade on 17/08/07.

Chapter 23

TEMPLATE FOR REGIONAL DEVELOPMENT

Manding Medical Centre became a template for districts elsewhere and villagers to nurture, develop further and handover to the next generation. This None Governmental Health Organization epitomizes a developmental watchtower for the region.

Manding medical center is a pulsating source of hope, jobs training and superb medical service at Njawara village the Gambia. Everyone knows that government alone does not move things fast enough. Society must be radical and pragmatic to pitch into its development.

We know all too well that the developed world got where its because private efforts were self prophetic and projects like Manding Medical Centre goes long ways to initiate and stimulate community to work together for a positive agenda for its people.

Hence after many years of foot dragging and vicissitude by society I decided I will build the hospital if I have to single-handed. I worked years receiving no government assistance and without grants from the great of the Gambian community.

Dr. Alhasan Sisawo Ceesay, MD

Manding Medical Centre is a positive good that help our regions to cross the road to a better healthcare delivery. We thank every one for making it possible that our center became a platform and guide in rejuvenating our regions. We now provide medical service to all Gambians and none Gambians domiciled in the Gambia. We will create more jobs as need arises.

This was the reason why I gave my life's comfort for reward that will benefit most needy villagers. It came through determination and kindness of many people worldwide.

There are some things only governments can do but together communities through collective initiatives can achieve at least fifty percent of their developmental needs in addition to government effort.

Today some see Manding medical centre as perpetual monument of good, an honor to the country and a general benefit to villagers and children in the North Bank of the Gambia. Manding medical centre is an inspiration and cause for thankfulness and celebration.

Miss Roheyata Ceesay, Daughter

Dr. Alhasan Sisawo Ceesay, MD

Chapter 24

AN APPEAL TO INTERNATIONAL COMMUNITY

Dear Readers,

The above information about Manding Medical Centre is included in this work only hoping that it will help spread the word more extensively and draw awareness to a greater community of people and readers of my work. It's my belief that lots of good people out there may want to participate or give to the cause and goal of the center should they be aware of its existents for the villagers. Hence, I am appealing for help and participatory support from all able to extend their hearts to make this much needed medical endeavor to come to fruition for the rural sector of the Gambia. Who knows you might even end up coming to bask in our beautiful seaside and relish Gambian generosity. Music for me is reaching out to help others and my patients are yearning for your kind participation and donation in cash/kind. Thanks a million for considering our appeal. God blesses your heart(s). I write with believe that by it money can be generated to provide a much needed medical service to the rural sector. Writing about the Manding Medical Centre may course some Good Samaritan and any wanting to leave foot prints on the sand of time for a good cause to come to our assistance to help us meet the goals of the center at Njawara village, the Gambia, West Africa. My head, heart and soul are devoted to my family, the Gambia and Manding Medical Centre. It is not a God given calling but a mere conviction that our rural folks deserve better health service than currently available and hence human calling to want to contribute positively to bring resolution of some of our rural health service inadequacies. I never had an angel come down to me nor have I ever heard the voices of God saying, "Ceesay, you must do so and so" as many mocked Manding Medical Centre emanated from sheer conviction that it is a dutiful way of doing the right thing for curbing premature deaths of children before reaching 5 years of life from malaria, water born diseases, and warm infestations; and in the same vein providing both pre and postnatal care to the pregnant. Hence, portions of proceeds of sales in all my work go to help meet the center's operational costs and in providing scholarship to indigent indigenous rural candidates due course return to serve rural Gambia wishing to read for a medical degree or agriculture and Medicine.

Signed: Dr. Alhasan S. Ceesay, MD/Email: alhasanceesay@hotmail.com

Dr. Alhasan Sisawo Ceesay, MD

Chapter 25

LORNA ROBINSON, AN ANGEL OF MERCY

Keith, Dr. Ceesay, & late Lorna Robinson

There are certain moulds God broke them moments after He finished making them. Mrs. Lorna V. Robinson was one of these unique, caring, sharing and rare angels of mercy. Mrs. Lorna Robinson and I met through her job as general nurse at the then Essex County General hospital in Colchester, Essex County in 1990, when I was a trainee doctor at the hospital.

She and husband Keith Robinson became my friends as far back as in the 1990s and one of their annual pilgrimages is visiting my family in the Gambia, West Africa.

This benevolent couple has since been my Colchester if not my England. Together we set to catch a dream of providing medical aid and service to Gambian villagers. I left at the end of my training to serve my country in 1992. In December 1999 Mrs. Lorna Robinson sent an invitation for my wife and I to attend wedding of Miss Fiona Robinson, her younger daughter, to gentleman Reeves.

We have since 2000 worked acidulously to make the above goal come to fruition, especially for those in the rural sector of the North Bank Region of the Gambia. It was Lorna's joint effort with, nurses, Doctors Laurel Spooner, Barbara Murray, Richard Spooner, Phil Murray, Linda Mahon-Daly, Peter R. Wilson, Malkait Singh and residents of Colchester, which lead to the formation of the Colchester Friends of Manding Charitable Trust.

It was registered as a charity in England and Wales in 2001. The charity number is 1088136. This charity acts as liaison in the European Union countries for Manding Medical Centre at Njawara village in the Badibous of the North Bank Region, the Gambia.

Since its conception, the Friends of Manding Charitable Trust had busied itself on weekly or bimonthly Gambi-barzaars in an effort to help raise money for building of both the children and maternity units of the center. Mrs. Lorna Robinson spent countless week-ends either selling material such as toys, coats and anything she could lay her hands on as long as she believes it will generate money for the building of the children and maternity units of the center. She spent most of her retirement time organizing activity for the center to help promote our cause. She sent books, spectacles, pens and pencils along with medication for the center's use.

The influence of this Good Samaritan group in Colchester reverberated and lead to the formation of a similar charity group in America, which is lead by Dr. Avery Aten, Alpena Friends of Manding Charitable Trust, Michigan, USA, was formed in May 2005.

All this came about because Mrs. Lorna V. Robinson, the lady of mercy behind the wheel, would not rest while the indigent goes without the most basic things in life. Here is how Lorna views her part during one of many conversations we had about the need to share worth and ourselves with other less fortunate than us.

She simply said, "Ceesay, I feel delighted and warm at heart in helping others, like the villagers. I strongly belief good used could be made from my work and experience I had at the NHS over years. I will try to recruit as many retired nurses to our cadre as long as they listen to my please. The other secrete is that such activity keeps me young, participating and contributing to the needy. I feel alive and forever growing. In life we most extend our hearts to others and with compassion reach the needy." This tit bit tells about the unselfish nature of Mrs. Lorna V. Robinson who through the years since her retirement gave her all to help others, especially the villagers, breath a sigh of relief and to have hope and knowledge that someone far away they never met cared about them.

Lorna continued saying, "It brings joy to my heart when I share the little I have with the needy. It helps to uplift the despondent. Millions suffer needlessly for not having means of proper health care, clean and safe water, good shelter and chance to attend schools. I want to help you get the villagers from a downward spiral of deepening health deprivation.

I certainly take hope in people like you and your stand to help your folks back home in the Gambia."

It was this unique caring angel that I lost on the third of March 2010 for she returned peacefully to her maker on this day. The above was my Lorna and now I cry, when shall we be blessed will another like her? Losing Lorna Robinson left me feeling that I lost the best person, outside of my family, I ever known. She was a kind soul of unswerving determination to share the little She had with the little guy needing her help. She stood by my cause in thick and thin moments of my stay in the United Kingdom.

Dr. Alhasan S. Ceesay graduating from the American University of the Caribbean, West Indies, 1992

The provision of medical care to villagers is more than a responsibility; it is a sacred trust for me. I will not the villagers or memory Mrs. Lorna V. Robinson down because I believe in looking to the well being of the less fortunate. One carries on trying on reflecting on all the children and villagers who need this health care. Hence no trepidation will hold me back.

My family, the villagers and I miss and deeply mourn her premature departure from mother earth. May she rest in peace with her maker and may we the living without fail or fear able to follow the high shining examples of indefatigable Good Samaritan she was in life.

I hope you will join me to keep her memory and legacy alive for other to copy while we continue taking medical aid to villagers in rural Gambia. Lorna V. Robinson thanks a million and goodbye for now.

Signed: Dr. Alhasan S. Ceesay, MD

Manding Medical Centre, Njawara

The Gambia, West Africa. E-mail: alhasanceesay@hotmail.com

Chapter 27

I REST MY CASE

Paul in a letter to Timothy 2 said, "I have fought a good fight, I have finished my course, and I have kept the faith." I hand this work for publication for you to be judge of the ravages of the years and how my life was that of extreme ups and downs.

In reality, I am very grateful to God even though my life met with various misfortunes, the most unbearable being the delay in my becoming a physician.

My life as witnessed in these pages was an assembly of trials and tribulation emanating from roadblocks placed on my path by inhuman laws and unfortunate dark circumstances.

Life has taught me to submit to divine decrees, whatever they may be from God. I feel on the whole overly rewarded and delivered even though I had no family here in England nor was I as lucky as others who can feel and experience the warmth of their wives and children on daily basis.

I succumbed to it as the way things were going to be for me and lived with this state of affairs while in Manchester, England. I experienced various turns of fate, enough for ten elephant loads, while on the little moat of the silver sea called England.

With my travels I was able to see Europe, the Americas and have learnt a great deal from it as well as experienced numerous unforeseen adventures thrown on my path. My life in England was pain; fear of deportation, hunger, extreme poverty due to joblessness, solitude and missing my wife and children I loved dearly. I had a huge sense of duty in relation to the villagers and was not ready to fail them because of personal comfort or pleasures.
Consequently Manding Medical Centre and benefits to be accrued from it became my most if not the only occupation and direction in life.
Here is Manding Medical Centre if managed well it will do justice to rural health service for the next generation of Gambians to build upon.The medical centre is now a recognized charity in both the United Kingdom and America. I am committed to serve the villagers so that life of the children and young people would be better than mine when I was young.
I hope Manding Medical Centre becomes a model testimony of the boy from Njawara village who doggedly struggled to become a doctor and despite various twists of life is able to provide medical aid and service to villagers in rural Gambia.May be this will strengthen some other fellow to strive to do better than I did to bring health and happiness to the region. I hope my adventure persuades youngsters that man is capable of a lot more than he thinks he is capable of.

Dr. Alhasan Sisawo Ceesay, MD

Our footprints must be inspirational to give heart to new coming Gambian generations. Twenty years ago none would dream of thinking me becoming an author or to challenge powers as I did in this little frame and life of mine. I met a beautiful Maraka girl while I was in Monrovia, Liberia, West Africa. Fatou Koma is daughter of Elhaj Ansuman Koma and Jalian Ture of Kindia from Guinea Conakry.

Her positive attitudes towards me lead our meeting on weekends at Cousin Sainabou Jobe's home. We started going out together and very soon I had the courage to ask her hand in marriage. There was no bone of contention with regards for my love for her. She was the darling of my heart at first sight and I was not going to let a fly land on her from that day onwards.

We had a simple wedding because her father did not quite approve of me because of fear for his uneducated but very pretty daughter being dump at one stage of the marriage for another educated city girl.

I, in the long run, allied his fears and he ended up being one of my best friends and confidants I had up to the day he went to his maker.

Fatou Koma-Ceesay and I are blessed with three beautiful daughters namely, Princesses Famatanding Ceesay, Binta Ceesay, and Roheyata Ceesay. All of who, unlike me, had their schooling start at the age of five. The elder girl is aspiring to become a doctor and had been admitted to start her premed courses at Alpena Community College in Alpena, Michigan, USA.

Together Fatou Koma-Ceesay, the children and I went through all the tragedy of hunger, poverty and other sad experiences my sojourn in the quest of the Golden flees for the villager brought to us. Fatou Koma-Ceesay initially hated Manding Medical Centre for she felt it consumed me and took me away from her and the children. The call got me entangled in a web of unfortunate circumstances and laws.

The marriage had at one point almost spiralled to its end as wife' move became questionable. Nonetheless she remained a good mother and wife who took care of the girls in my absence.

My mother in-law was battered by confusion and as to why Fatou stuck it out with me under such immense hardship. Love is stronger glue! We loved each other and so we were able to stand by the other in good or bad times and my trip to England was the worst ever in our connubial life.

It caused great turbulences in the marriage but I stuck with it for love's shake and the children who I love dearly.

Today, we are back together as family under the same roof while planning and supporting future of our darling girls.

God bless Fatou Koma-Ceesay's heart and be reassured of endless love I have for her.

For now Dalliance said it best for me when he said, "Say of me what you will and the morrow will judge you, and your words shall be a witness before its judgment and a testimony before it justice.

Dr. Alhasan Sisawo Ceesay, MD

I came to say a word and I shall utter it. Should death take me ere I give voice; the morrow shall utter it. That which alone I do today shall be proclaimed before the people in days to come." I wrote with the hope the life enshrined herein will serve not only as an inspiration to the despondent but a lesson never to allow this sort of experience it passed through this planet.

I wrote in the hope that life enshrined in my books will serve not only as an inspiration to the despondent and downtrodden but a lesson never to allow this sort of experience it passed through this planet. I wrote because I felt that my life has something worth revealing to the world to engender tolerance and understanding between people and their governments.

I risked revealing today for all of us to learn from it and move to a better and rewarding future.Among the forces of life is one that stands a certain lofty peak a few is endowed with or able to explore its heights. Ambition urges us to leave the lower surface of earth where the ordinary people live and ascend to heights that pierce the heavens.

This mission has led to numerous Erie paths but for me this Pell-mell towards a better medical service for the neglected villager was a worthwhile adventure.

I am profoundly grateful and indebted to my wife Fatou Koma-Ceesay and our daughters, princesses Famatanding Ceesay, Binta Ceesay and Roheyata Ceesay for enduring all the pains that we went through in thick and thin times during my sojourn to America and England.

Also my deepest gratitude goes to Cousin Yata Sey-Corr for helping keep my family hopeful. God bless her heart eternally. I forgive my own brothers and sisters who refused to cater for my family in my absence. Hello, hats off to Sey kunda!

Dr. Alhasan Ceesay, holding Africa

Dr. Alhasan Sisawo Ceesay, MD
Chapter 28

MY ENDEARING LIFE & FATE

For a while in my native innocence all I had was erudition and wit, which always misfired. Everything I touched came to nothing but failure, whatever I tried to achieve came crashing down on my head. At any given moment some mishap befalls me and nothing surprised me any more. I took my current plight with stride and smiled as fate taunts me. I remain poor but my in extinguishable strong will enabled me face life squarely and took me through these dark days. The twist of fate abated but my age had advanced beyond retrieval. The above apocalyptic life is indeed trying moments for my family and me. The only passion I have is providing medical service to villagers through Manding Medical Centre. My dream spawns better future health service for future generations. I never set to write a bestseller but to inform and share ideas. Also I enjoy reading it as it's not found in any bookstore. It is hoped that in writing another will be spared of experienced I endured before being able to provide medical service/aid to Gambian villagers. Browse: http://friendsofmandinggambimed.btck.co.uk or contact alhasanceesay@hotmail.com

To view/purchase books: Google search Dr. Alhasan Ceesay/ books.

Chapter 28

THE WAY OF

A DREAMER

Back in the Gambia a friend decried my efforts as nothing but a dream that I persistently chased. I let such observers know that it only takes time before my dream become fruitful. Here are a few examples: I left the Gambia in 1967 as a nurse and returned; after insurmountable roadblocks as a medical doctor. While practicing in the Gambia I further created two worthy entities, namely (1) The Gambia Health Credit Union, which today provides needed financial assistance to all health workers i.e. Nurses and Health Inspectors country wide. (2) In addition I created NGO Manding Medical Centre at Njawara village, Lower Badibou to help provide a much needed medical aid and service free of charge to villagers who could not afford to pay private clinics. With the help of visiting doctors the centre has treated more than 9000 villagers free of charge since its inception in 1993.

On returning to the UK, I again with help of resident nurses and doctors in Colchester Essex setup the Friends of Manding Charitable trust in Colchester UK. This was recognized and registered as a charity in England and Wales by the UK- charity Commission in 2002.

Dr. Alhasan Sisawo Ceesay, MD

In the midst of which I published my first book 'The Legend Against all Odds' and now has published more than thirty eight novels. To further cement my goal for the villager I was able to convince the Alpena City Council to form a sister city link with Njawara and Kinte Kunda villages in the Lower Badibous of the Gambia in 2005. This was made easier after my being awarded on May 5th, 2005 'Distinguished Graduate Award' by Alpena Community College. My web site: friends of Manding gambimed continues to lure people to Njawara to see what help they could give the villager.

Today, I am not only an author of several books; Google search: Dr. Alhasan Ceesay/books to view of purchase as contribution to rural healthcare; portions or sales from these books go to support goals of Manding medical Centre at Njawara. I am indeed a dreamer and will continue to dream fir my people. If the above is dream then here is another step to help see through me.

I am humble to let you know I am now a Publisher and my company in the UK is 'PUBLISH KUNSA LTD' and one can have their work published by logging on to our web site; www.publishkunsa.com. Again two pounds sterling from any book published by my company goes towards scholarships and rural healthcare as stipulated in terms of contract we would work on manuscripts. Dreams must be activated and not wasted.

I cannot fly without wing but can make artificial wings to let reach higher hits that loafers never can dream of. Allow the dream to force you into action. Yes, I too have a dream, which is simply that every hamlet in the Gambia be bequeathed good healthcare, safe drinking water, enough food and chance to a solid education for every child.

Yes. Education is power and a mover. I sacrificed my life to endure depravity, humiliation and solitude in other to bring medical aid to villagers. With all these I am busy trying to get more medical skills and experience before heading to Gambia, home , sweet home.

With this tit-bit I can freely and willingly encourage you to dream but not to let it remain at that. A life with trials or challenge is like an orchestra without conductor and it very defeating if not boring indeed. One must act for the good of self and any community we find our selves.

An old village sage once advice that 'A good person and at best a leader never yield to failure but only learns from it to move forward. Grand Pa Bajoja Ceesay told me that; "One willing to do good should not expect people to remove obstacles or stones from their path; but such leaders must accept it calmly in the event these place more boulders on our way."This is what a dream turns out. At first it becomes a lonely avenue full of heartaches, which eases gradually as the good things unfold from one's relentless efforts to make the dream becomes fruitful and rewarding.

Simple its life 99.9% very hard work full of stumbling. Do not we all dream of going to heaven? Well the path to such respites need challenging theological and spiritual discipline. Hence we earthly dreamers dabble with ideas of landing on Mars and eventually colonizing it. So allow me ask, what is your dream for mankind, especially Africa?

Can Africa ever be free of ignorance, self subtenant, corruption and misuse of the tribe? These just few multipronged toxic dragon heads African must dream to remove from our midst. With better education and discipline Africa can overcome and progress. Dreamers are doing utmost to slay the pestilent dragon hindering life in the villages of rural Africa.

We must remove the monster of retro ration for the shake of the future generation. Again grandpa Bajoja Ceesay advices that we stay the good cause and never be taken by detractions. I am no millionaire but have a million dreams worthy of pursuing for my people. Would you dream along with me? Glad to let you know hard work yields rewarding fruits.

Dream and be in control of not only your own life but be a source of hope and inspiration while contributing positively to your community. Do not be carried along by current get rich quick and live selfishly. Life is to be shared even with dreamers. Time is not mine and life will continue for the villager. Success comes slowly and brings with it contagious hope that serves as blue print for other.

Njawara Banti Yassin

The fate of mankind is up to each of us. Do not succumb to idleness. Use youthful opportunity to develop out of ignorance, and corruption by having courage to bring change to the people. Be the change you want in others. Expect resistance on your path to bring change.

A useful proxy in fulfilling a dream is not letting it wane away. Always think it possible and work hard at its realization. Be warned to think what could be done and not that which cannot be archived. Matrix of success lies in hard work with guided ski full knowledge.

I will work on my dream and morrow will be my judge along with benefits accrued from it. I hope my last footprints of my journey on earth will inspire people towards doing well and sharing their worth with others. From one villager to another may this wish be true for rural Gambia.

Dr. Alhasan Sisawo Ceesay, MD

Chapter 30

ABOUT THE AUTHOR

I was born at Njawara Village, Lower Badibou District in the North Bank of the Gambia. I am a scion of a Mandinka and Fulani tribe and am one of five siblings. I had my education at Kinte Kunda, then Armitage High School, ending up as a registered nurse at the Royal Victoria Hospital, Banjul, before embarking to the USA on my medical degree quest.

I graduated from the American University School of Medicine in Montserrat, West Indies, in 1992 and returned to the Gambia to start setting up a self-help village health NGO Manding Medical Centre. The Gambia Government and the Badibou local authority register NGO Manding Medical Centre. The centre has treated more than 9000 patients free. I am married to Fatou Koma-Ceesay and we are blessed with three beautiful girls, Famatanding Ceesay, Binta Ceesay and Roheyata Ceesay.

Unlike me, all of them started school early without the roadblocks I had to cross in my early years. I am currently a medical officer at the Royal at the Royal Victoria Hospital on study leave. It is my hope that this work will inspire others and bring much needy help to providing medical service to rural Gambia.

You are urged to log onto: www.friendsofmanding gambimed.btck.co.uk, to learn more about my work with villagers. Dear reader I hope you enjoyed navigating through the piece of work I am contribute for all of us makes case for change in attitudes of government and the governed. For now, Dalliance said it best for me when he said, "Say of me what you will and the morrow will judge you, and your words shall be a witness before its judgment and a testimony before its justice. I came to say a word and I shall utter it. Should death take me ere I give voice, the morrow shall utter it. That which alone I do today shall be proclaimed before the people in days to come."

 I wrote with the hope the life and position enshrined herein will serve as not only an inspiration to farmers, the despondent but also a lesson never to allow these shameful international jigsaw games continue as experience to pass through this planet.

 I felt that it is worth writing about the above because it is something worth revealing to honorable men and women to engender change, tolerance and understanding between people and governments. I risked speaking out for all of us to learn from it and move forward to a better and rewarding future.

Have your manuscript become a book by submitting it for possible publication to acquisitions@publish Kunsa. Com

PLease contact us to expose your work globally.

PUBLISH KUNSA.COM

Dr, Alhasan Sisawo Ceesay, MD

Dr. Alhasan S. Ceesay graduating from the American
University of the Caribbean School of Medicine 1992

Njawara Banti Yassin

Keith, Dr. Ceesay, and Mrs. Lorna Robinson

Dr. Alhasan Sisawo Ceesay, MD

Miss Binta Ceesay, Daughter

Miss Roheyata Ceesay, Daughter

L – R: Dr. Alhasan Ceesay, Prof. Sulayman Nyang,

Mr. Clloyd Ramsey and Prof. Francis Conti

Dr. Alhasan Sisawo Ceesay, MD

Dr. Alhasan S. Ceesay holding Africa

Dr. Ceesay displays first book: The

Legend Against All Odds, Published 2002